JUST ONE RULE

EMILY ALTER

Copyright © 2025 by Emily Alter

All rights reserved.

No part of this book may be reproduced in any form or by any electronic or mechanical means, including information storage and retrieval systems, without written permission from the author, except for the use of brief quotations in a book review.

Edited by Jennifer Griffin.

Cover Design by Temptation Creations.

JUST ONE RULE

Eli

I knew what I wanted. What I wanted hadn't included losing the last connection I had with my biological family, but I still knew what I wanted.

I wanted Mistress Erika. I wanted to be owned, to be in the kind of 24/7 dynamic we fantasized about every time we spent together at the local BDSM club She'd founded.

Erika

I barely recognized Eli when they showed up at my door, soaked and on the verge of a breakdown.

On paper, Eli would be the perfect sub to soothe the high protocol Domme in me, but theory wasn't always everything. Everyone knew me as the Domme who was ten steps ahead at any given time, the one who hatched a million different plans to keep everyone together, and safe, and happy.

Even if all Eli was asking of me was one rule, it felt like more. I didn't know what that more would entail, or how to give it to them.

Just One Rule includes 24/7 Total Power Exchange, many rubber suits, a bad case of dom drop that was a long time coming if we were honest, group play, broken hearts and messy attachment styles, a kind of chaotic found family, a sub who isn't aware of how well they actually handle stress, and healing through a humiliation kink (and therapy).

KINKS INCLUDED IN JUST ONE RULE

- 24/7 Total Power Exchange
- Age play (mentioned)
- Domestic servitude
- Electro-play
- Exhibitionism
- Fisting
- Group play
- Humiliation
- Impact play (single tail whip)
- Leather (mentioned)
- M/s
- Objectification
- Orgasm control
- Puppy play
- Rubber
- Sensory deprivation
- Sex toys (Hitachi wands, violet wands, machines)
- Voyeurism

CONTENT WARNINGS

- **Family trauma**. Eli is kicked out by their uncle (only relative they still had a relationship with), and that trauma is processed throughout the book.
- **International adoption** (mentioned). Erika was adopted as a baby by white parents.
- **Sex work**. Eli engages in online sex work as a side hustle (live cams). It is mentioned that Erika used to work as a Professional Dominatrix.

GLOSSARY

- **Plumas**: feathers. Pluma is also used to say someone "looks gay/fem" (mostly used when referring to queer men). For reference, plumo-fobia means fem-phobia.
- **VIPS**: it's a chain restaurant and the closest to an American diner you can find in Spain. *And* it's famous for letting you stay as long as you want, and having chargers available on demand.

1

ELI

Rain kept falling against the pavement, ricocheting off the grey surface. The sound thrummed through my ears, a migraine building. I rang the buzzer again.

I was completely soaked. It had been raining all day, but I hadn't been thinking. It was only a drizzle when I walked out —when I was forced out.

I pressed the buzzer again, over and over. I didn't understand. I didn't know what to do if She didn't respond.

I knew Erika wasn't at the gym—it was too late at night. All the lights were off and the shutters were down. But I heard Erika say once that She had an app on Her phone, and She got alerts if someone was at the door, trying to get in.

I stifled a whimper. My body felt cold, freezing, but my face burned with tears. I didn't know when those had started. My stomach cramped. I wasn't sure if it was hunger or a reaction to the cold.

Panic started taking precedence over the numbness and the dread.

I couldn't sleep outside. I wouldn't survive. I wouldn't know where to start looking, what to do.

I didn't know if this town even had a homeless shelter, or if one would even be safe. TV shows and movies said they weren't.

I banged my hands against the metal shutters.

Sobs racked my body. I had no clue what to do. I didn't have anyone's address. The club was closed because we couldn't justify having it open every day. Only Thursdays to Sundays. I'd heard Erika say She wanted to change that, but it hadn't happened yet.

The only address I knew, other than the club, was the gym.

I couldn't even remember why I knew it. Probably because Erika had mentioned running the gym, and I'd been curious about it, too intrigued not to try and learn more about Her.

Shit.

I was alone.

Truly alone.

My phone had died hours ago, and I didn't have a charger or access to a bank account. I couldn't reach out to anyone.

I let my knees hit the ground. The pain was immediate—nothing like the thud and the sting that followed when I kneeled for a Domm. This wasn't a pain I wanted to chase—a shock to my system that led to everything quieting down, to peace settling over my bones.

Could I go to an ER?

My teeth chattered. I wiped at my cheeks. Hospitals were overworked, but maybe they could point me in the right direction. They had social workers, too.

Right.

That would mean knowing where the nearest ER was, and the rain didn't stop. At least here I wasn't fully exposed to the weather, the eave providing a thin semblance of coverage.

"Hey!" I flinched. That wasn't Erika. I tried to shift back, to hide. There was no point. The footsteps kept coming closer, faster. They were heavy. I should run, but I was frozen, stuck. "Fuck. Eli?"

Uh?

I looked up through bleary eyes. Maybe I hadn't reacted because deep down I'd recognized the voice. Abel, Erika's friend, was hovering over me, wielding a large blue umbrella.

He was Sergio's Daddy, an ex-firefighter who now worked at the gym with Erika, but I didn't interact with him a lot.

Then again, I didn't interact with many people outside of Erika. Sometimes María. She was good at handling me, too.

"Eli?" He squatted down. I bit my lip. I wanted to say something, but I didn't know what. Words had always been hard. "Hey. What are you doing here?"

I swallowed. My fingers curled. I wanted to talk, to explain, I just—

Abel moved until he could cover us both with the umbrella. It had little bubbles, so I assumed it was Sergio's. Sergio was obsessed with octopi and all sea creatures, and he was a Little. The umbrella fit him more than it fit his Daddy.

"Do you need to go to a hospital, Eli?" The rain now ricocheted against the plastic above us. The sound was too loud, too thunderous. Too distracting. "You look like you're in shock."

I shook my head. I didn't feel quite grounded, but I didn't think I was too out of it, either. If I thought really hard about it, there was nothing to be shocked about. It had just been a matter of time.

"M-Mistress?" I pushed the word out.

My voice sounded weak to my own ears, weaker than it normally did.

I closed my eyes. I didn't know if I could say it again if he didn't get what I was saying.

"Erika asked me to drive by," Abel said. Hearing Her

name helped me focus. My body was a live wire, completely tuned to him. "The cameras are glitching. We're waiting for someone to repair them, but she kept getting notifications on her app that someone might be trying to get in."

"Sorry." I swallowed once, twice. It didn't get rid of the bitter taste in my mouth.

"Did you want to see her?" Abel cocked his head to the side.

I couldn't resent him. He was still new to the community. He wasn't at Plumas every day or have brunch with us every Sunday. He wouldn't know about how I struggled to communicate verbally. Words were lead past my tongue, sticky and heavy and overwhelming.

I nodded. I didn't want to see pity, or frustration, or… anything in his face, so I kept my face down, eyes on the dirty pavement. More than anything, I didn't want to see him shaking his head, ready to tell me it wasn't possible to see Erika.

"You know she's going to make you go to a hospital the second she lays eyes on you, right?"

It didn't matter. Erika made everything better. I would do anything She wanted, anything She asked of me. I just needed a second to breathe. She gave me that, always.

Seconds passed, then Abel stood up and sighed. "Okay, then. Let me help you up."

I took his hand easily. He acted as if I was going to break, as if touching me would be the trigger. I didn't mind touch. He could touch me. It didn't make a difference, didn't change anything. Erika trusted him, so I did too.

It was too late, and I was too exhausted to dissect that thought further. I just let him guide me to his car—Sergio's car? They'd once talked about bringing all his things from Madrid, but I couldn't remember if that had included a car. Or maybe the car had already been here. I didn't know.

He'd left the heating of the seats on. The contrast made me want to jump and move away. Before he'd taken a turn out of the street, though, I was already sinking to the heat, my eyes closing as I grew drowsy. I'd walked all day before I remembered I could try Erika's gym.

I was tired.

"Siri, call Erika." Abel's voice boomed in the car. He usually had a soft voice, so it had me turning toward him. I was in the passenger seat. It was strange. Most people plopped me in the back and called it a day. The call rang a few times before it connected. There was static for a second before Abel spoke again. I fidgeted. I'd been hoping to hear Erika's voice. "Er, I have Eli in the car. We're driving to your place."

Two beats passed. "Eli?"

"I think they're in shock, but they won't let me take them to a hospital without seeing you first."

"Okay," Erika said. "Are you on speaker?"

"I just said I'm driving."

"Fuck off, Eeyore." I jolted. I wasn't used to hearing Erika curse. I knew She was joking around, but it was still shocking. "Wait for me downstairs. No point in coming up if we're heading out again."

"Yes, Ma'am."

"Very funny."

The call hung up after that. I looked away, through the window. I didn't realize, but I'd been holding my breath. I didn't have a plan, didn't know what to do once Erika was in front of me. I didn't know how She'd react to my banging on the door to Her gym. Maybe She wasn't happy. Maybe She didn't approve.

I should've thought of something else, something smarter. Maybe a server in a VIPS would've lent me a charger, and I could've asked someone to meet me there and cover the tab.

I *was* hungry, so that would've been smarter.

I just... I didn't think.

Again.

The rest of the drive passed in a blur. Abel didn't try to make conversation, but I caught him glancing my way every now and then, drumming a random rhythm against the steering wheel.

I squirmed but tried to hide it. I wasn't sure I was successful.

It didn't matter.

Abel stopped in front of a nondescript building that looked like it had been built in the past decade. It was too polished and sharp. Not too much it stuck out like a sore thumb, but it didn't blend in completely with all the old buildings that the north of Spain was famous for.

The wide glass doors opened one second later. Well, realistically, more time probably passed. It didn't matter. The doors opened, and Erika ran to us. She had an umbrella, too, one of those clear ones. I used to have one like that.

Erika opened the door to the passenger seat. I gasped, a mixed response to the sight of Her and the sudden shift in temperature.

She placed a hand on my cheek. It was hard not to break down when She did that. Maybe Abel had been on to something. My eyes smarted, my breath picking up.

"Eli, I need you to tell me what happened."

"Er, get inside and close the door," Abel said from behind me. "They can tell you while we're driving."

I shook my head. My fingers itched to lean forward, to touch. No, She couldn't get away. She'd just arrived. She was close here. I could feel Her presence, the warmth I bathed in whenever I saw Her.

"Shush," Erika said to Abel before Her focus shifted back to me. "Are you hurt?"

Yes.

No.

I shivered. I didn't know how to explain it. It was all too much. A whimper slipped past my lips. It was not going to fly with Erika. Erika was the person who pushed me the hardest to use words. Not in the way therapists did, but She didn't spend too much time trying to guess what I was trying to say or put words in my mouth.

Maybe She'd make an exception tonight.

She didn't push me because She couldn't guess, anyway. I didn't know how She did it, but every time I said something, She seemed to have been ready for it, to have known.

"My k-knees." My teeth chattered.

Abel might've been on to something else, asking Her to close the door.

"What about your knees?" Erika's gaze darted down.

Obviously, we both knew She couldn't see through my clothes, but that didn't stop the shiver running down my spine. She pretended not to see it, not to react to it.

"Fell."

I whimpered. Adrenaline and dissociation had kept me from feeling the full sting. Now the sharp pain, the throbbing of bruises forming—there was probably blood, too—had me on the verge of tears.

"They were on their knees when I arrived," Abel explained. "Crying."

My lips parted. I didn't know what sound I wanted to make or what words I wanted to say. Erika cupped my cheek with Her hand. Back when we'd first met, I'd realized that I liked the contrast in our skins, Her dark brown to my pasty white. The first time I played with Her and realized how my heart beat quicker when I focused on our intertwined fingers, I'd gone down a rabbit hole of research.

The conclusion I reached was that my reaction was no stronger than when I caught myself staring at María's freckles, or the tattoos on León and Danny.

"Did you fall on the ground?"

I blinked. Erika had Her eyes on me. Her hair was in braids that went past Her chest, pulled back with a wide headband. Had She been sleeping? I'd never been to Her apartment. I didn't know anything about Her routines other than the few details She let slip while we were at the club.

I swallowed. "Yes."

Erika was going to have follow-up questions. Raindrops got into the car as a gust of wind whipped my face.

There were too many things.

"Okay, before that, did anyone hurt you?"

"Do you need to do this now, Er?" Abel's voice had a grumbling quality.

He used that voice when he pretended to scold Sergio. They were sweet together.

"They're too overstimulated as it is," Erika said to him. I breathed out. If they talked amongst themselves, I didn't have to focus. "We need to know what the fuck to tell the triage nurse because Eli won't be able to."

I chewed on my lip. It was cold. Erika was right, though. There was also the fact that I didn't want to go to the hospital to begin with. I didn't want to fight Her—either of them, however.

"At least move to the back seat with them. We can hash out everything in the parking lot."

Silence grew. I didn't dare look up, but I guessed they were having some kind of silent contest. In the end, Erika sighed. "Okay."

"You are stubborn as fuck," Abel complained.

I frowned. I didn't think She was stubborn. Erika just knew what She was doing, all of the time. I admired that about Her.

"Let's go, pet."

"Yes, Mistress Erika."

2

ERIKA

Eli didn't complain as I moved them off the heated seat up front and helped them into the back seat. I dropped the umbrella on the floor there before turning my full attention on them. I was still trying to piece together everything.

I had to call the technician that hadn't showed up yet to fix the camera at the gym entrance, too. I didn't think it would've made a world of difference, but if I'd known it was Eli, I would've gone straight to them. I'd been on the phone with Abel when I started getting the notifications, and he was closer and struggling with insomnia, so he offered to check it out. We thought it would be a homeless person, or perhaps a random guy who'd drunk too much.

It happened.

"What were you doing out in the rain, Eli?"

I knew people said we up north didn't mind the rain, but there was a difference between not using an umbrella when it was drizzling, and this. It was almost suicidal. Eli didn't always care for their body, but they weren't usually this reckless.

A shiver ran down their spine—another one. I was keeping track. Abel was right in having been impatient with me, but I knew Eli. They were opening up more and more with me. We'd found a rhythm of sorts that worked to get them talking, but it was a thin line to tread, especially in emergencies.

I still didn't know if this constituted an emergency. I only knew Eli's skin was gelid to the touch, and there was a faraway look in their eyes.

"I need a place to stay," Eli mumbled.

They tried to hide their hands in the sleeves of the soaked, oversized hoodie they had on.

I should've brought them a change of clothes. Eli was shorter than I was, not as muscular, but at least they'd be dry. I hadn't known what to expect, though, if the clothes they were in would be needed as evidence of something.

This wasn't the time.

Eli needed a place to stay?

I went through everything I knew about their life outside of the club. It wasn't as much as I'd like, but it was more than any other person at Plumas would know about them.

"Something happened with your uncle?"

After coming out as nonbinary, most of Eli's family had turned their backs on them. Eli lived with one of their uncles while they finished culinary school. As of a few months ago, they had graduated, but their living situation hadn't changed. I'd tried to ask, but they hadn't been very forthcoming. I just knew that they wanted to be a personal chef instead of working somewhere like a crowded restaurant with people fighting to talk all over each other. They had really struggled during their internships, so I didn't blame them.

Eli chewed on their lip and glanced away.

I frowned. Eli was not the kind of sub to look away, even if the context right now was the furthest it could possibly be from kink. They definitely did not look away from me. I didn't care that it made me sound cocky.

Their hair was buzzed short and dyed to a sea green color I knew they changed constantly. It was strange to see them in bulky, oversized clothes when I was used to seeing them in rubber that clung to their skin, though. Many of us met for brunch on Sundays after spending Saturday at the club, and I dragged Eli with me at least half of the time. I still saw them in full gear more often than out of it. Much more often, actually.

Before I could further contemplate the differences between Eli in and out of kink, a sob slipped past their lips, racking through their entire body. Abel exchanged a worried glance with me in the rearview mirror. I'd consider how much I told him later.

"He found my... site."

Fuck.

Putting two and two together after that wasn't hard. Eli's entire family had already disowned them. If the uncle had been waiting for a reason, a spicy website Eli used to finance their last years of culinary school would've done it. And it would leave Eli with nothing. And no one. At least, no one blood related.

"He kicked you out," I stated for Abel's benefit more than Eli's. "And you went to the gym?"

I couldn't remember where the uncle's apartment was. I asked for an address when someone signed up to be a member of Plumas, but I'd never had an excuse to memorize it. I'd never driven them back, or picked them up, or even showed up with soup when they were sick like I did with some of the others.

Eli never asked, and they mentioned once it wasn't possible with their uncle in the apartment.

I should've pushed harder.

"Not at first." Eli sniffled. "I felt numb."

I nodded. I kept calculating, chastising myself. "Why didn't you call, Eli?"

I didn't like the pained whimper that fell from their parted lips, but I needed to know. "Phone died."

Fuck.

"Did you take anything? Drugs? Pills?"

Eli wasn't an addict. I'd never heard of them using recreationally or for pain management. I still had to ask. Abel was about to get us into the parking lot of the hospital. Depending on their answer, I had half a mind of telling him to turn around. I didn't know that the ER was going to help when the main risk here was that Eli had caught a cold. They certainly wouldn't be a high priority, which would mean sitting down on a plastic chair for hours, in soaked clothes, when they could be taking a warm bath and riding it out under a pile of blankets in my place.

"N-no, Mistress Erika, I would never—"

"It's okay." I raised my hand to still them before they drove themselves into a panic attack. "Do you need to get a prescription refilled for psych meds or anything else?"

There was a clause when people became a member at Plumas that they needed to disclose if they were diabetic or had any cardiac disease or blood pressure issues. It was a matter of safety. However, I didn't cover everything. There was a fine line between wanting to ensure someone's safety and stripping them of their privacy.

"PrEP?"

Worst case scenario, I'd just refilled my prescription, so we could use that while they got it sorted out with their primary doctor.

"Anything else?" I double-checked.

Eli shook their head. They looked exhausted, their body

slumped against the leather seats. I didn't think I was going to get much more out of them tonight.

Speaking of... "When's the last time you ate?"

A shrug. That was all the response I got. That and Eli curling their arms around their stomach.

So, a while.

"Ab, turn around."

"Er." When were other Domms going to get it through their heads that their stern, gruff tones didn't work on me?

"Unless you're concerned with something I haven't covered, an ER isn't going to help more than drawing them a bath and wrapping them up in a blanket. But the latter is going to be much quicker."

If he said the ER was necessary, I'd drag Eli out. Before I got him working for me as a personal trainer, Abel had worked as a firefighter in Madrid, and he had a bunch of first aid courses under his belt. I trusted him. But if I was right, Eli needed a calm environment more than being prodded at by nurses and doctors.

After a few seconds, Abel grunted. "Let me park and give them a quick check over. But you are taking them to their primary doctor tomorrow."

"I will."

If nothing else, Eli needed to sort out a new PrEP prescription. It would be on their health card, but I doubted a pharmacy would just hand them a new bottle of pills for a controlled medication.

They might need to switch doctors, too. It was the logical step. They'd need to update their place of residency as well, and that meant a new health center.

> **ERIKA**
> Are you awake?

> **MÓNICA**
> Barely
>
> Something wrong?

> **ERIKA**
> Yes
>
> I know you don't deal with residential buildings, but you have contacts. Is there anything available you'd recommend?

> **MÓNICA**
> You bought your place five years ago
>
> And you complained a lot about the whole process

> **ERIKA**
> It's not for me

> **MÓNICA**
> … Please tell me this isn't one of your schemes

> **ERIKA**
> I don't know what you mean

OBVIOUSLY, I knew what she meant. Mónica ribbed me more than some of the brats at the club. She was also my best friend, though, and a construction manager. She'd helped me find the duplex I was in after I thought I was going to lose it trying to deal with rental sites and real estate agencies.

> **MÓNICA**
> Offering people a job is questionable enough already

> You are *not* going to buy someone a house
>
> Who is it for, anyway?

ERIKA

> Eli
>
> And I'm not buying it for them, I'm helping with the first installment

MÓNICA

> Why does Eli need a house?

I hesitated all of two seconds before I typed back. With anyone else, I would've dropped it, but Mónica and I shared everything. We kept each other in check and called each other out when need be. She didn't gossip, either. Her Little, and the club's biggest size queen, Kara, complained plenty about it whenever we met outside of the club.

ERIKA

> Their uncle kicked them out, didn't even let them pack a bag

MÓNICA

> Fuck
>
> Are they with you?

ERIKA

> They're taking a bath
>
> It's a long story, but can you ask around about the apartment?
>
> I want to have options

MÓNICA

> Sure
>
> Iván was talking about expanding to (re)include residential stuff. I'll ask if he's already got anything in the works

>   ERIKA
>
>   Thanks
>
> MÓNICA
>
> Let me know if you need anything else, okay?
>
> I'm guessing Eli won't be like Sergio or Kara and appreciate all of us showing up at your place, but we could set up something at the club
>
>   ERIKA
>
>   For sure

Eli definitely wouldn't. Kara and Sergio were the epitome of Little subs. Whenever they were sick or feeling sad for some reason, the best thing to do for them was show up at their place with takeout, blankets, and snuggles. Attention whores was the name of the game for them. They thrived and healed under the attention. Eli liked to be the center of attention when they were hidden under a layer of latex and deep in subspace, but not outside of it.

That didn't mean they didn't thrive in community.

I was musing over plans we could carry out at the club when the ding of a bell pulled me out of my head. Even though I'd wanted to stay in the bathroom with Eli, I hadn't wanted to overwhelm them more. I'd run the bath and left a bunch of folded clothes on one of the shelves and a bell one of the brats at the club had gifted me once as some sort of prank. It was made of the cheapest plastic, but it was still useful from time to time.

"Everything okay?" I asked as I knocked on the bathroom door.

I didn't wait for Eli's cue before opening the door. They were to use the bell if they needed anything, so it was implied that I could walk in.

Eli was in the tub, the water clearer than when I'd left them to it. My gaze darted down, tracking the naked expanse of skin. I didn't let myself linger, instead focusing on the worry on Eli's face. It wouldn't do. They'd stopped crying, which they'd started doing again once I'd said goodbye to Abel and they'd apologized to him for making him go out of his way with the failed ER trip. In any other circumstance, I would've laughed at Abel's face. I bet the man had never struggled so much not to unfurl his inner Daddy, full force.

There were still tear tracks down Eli's cheeks, their eyes puffy, the skin around their lips reddened. Their nose, too.

"What did you need, pet?"

I was aware of the thin line I was walking. The balance between not taking advantage of Eli when they were vulnerable—of not turning this into the kinky dynamic we usually dived into—and giving them something to hold on to.

"Didn't thank you." Eli cleared their throat. Their voice showed signs of all that crying too, the sound wet and muffled. "For helping me. Mistress."

I stood straight, my body rigid. That thin line was becoming more slippery by the second, and Eli hadn't been under my roof for even an hour.

The knowledge didn't stop me from cutting the distance between us. I squatted down, tilting their chin up. Eli's bottom lip wobbled.

"What's my job, Eli?" The poor sub just cocked their head to the side. I licked my lips, considering how to rephrase it. "When we first negotiated playing in the club, what did I say?"

I wiped a thumb across their cheek while they thought of an answer. The skin was too soft to the touch from all the tears, but at least they weren't cold anymore. Abel still said they might wake up with a temperature tomorrow, but I'd already made sure I was stocked up on meds.

"You're responsible for me."

I smiled. I knew I could count on Eli to reach that conclusion. "Exactly."

Eli nodded. Their gaze darted down. I didn't think they were uncomfortable with my touch, but they were uncomfortable with something.

I couldn't blame them.

It had been a long day.

"Mistress?"

I didn't let it show, but I had a feeling it was going to take me some time not to jump with worry when I heard the honorific phrased like that. There was so much fear, so much doubt.

"What is it?" As I asked, I raced through ten different alternatives, trying to guess the words Eli was trying to push out. I didn't like it when others did it—when they guessed everything Eli had to say—but these were extenuating circumstances. I had to believe that they were. "Do you want me to stay in here?"

It didn't mean I wasn't selfish. *I* wanted to stay here, to make sure that there were no more tremors running down their body. No more tears.

Eli gave a quick nod. I breathed out, but then they shook their head. I narrowed my eyes. I was going to take a step back when they started sitting up.

"I…" They paused, their eyes widening for a second. I wasn't going to point out the obvious, but I recognized that look. When they were more upset than usual, being verbal was more challenging, the words running away from them. They didn't like it, either. "Get out."

"All right."

Before they could beat themselves up, I pulled Eli to their feet easily. I noted how there were no tremors, only a subtle attempt to cover themselves. I'd known them for about four years, seeing them at the club and—more rarely—outside of it, but there were too many things about them I didn't know yet. For one thing, no matter how much I'd played with their body, I'd never seen them fully naked.

And I wasn't counting today as the first time.

What I did was help them out of the tub and wrap them up in one of the large fluffy towels I kept by the heater I'd splurged on when I bought this place. It was one of the best luxuries I'd invested in.

Eli stifled a moan as I rubbed the towel against their arms. They slumped forward but held themselves still inches away.

"You can touch me, pet."

The moan that left their lips was more obvious then. Their mouth rested against my collarbone. Eli didn't kiss, but they breathed more deeply, tension that had still lingered even after soaking in the bath leaving their body in waves.

I rubbed the fluffy material against it, drying them as quickly as I could. I knew them. They didn't need to tell me they didn't want me to go soft. It wasn't just about their role as a slave, or a sub, or an object. Drying them with the same care I would an object was about the relationship with their body. Eli didn't get a chance to worry about feelings of dysphoria if their body didn't get the treatment of a human body.

When the skin blossomed red in places, that was when I knew I was keeping them in the right headspace while looking out for them.

"I texted Mónica while you were in the bathtub," I said as I ran the towel down their legs. I had to place one of their hands on my shoulder first. Eli had good balance, but that was when they were actively focusing on it. "She knows you're with me, and she mentioned we could set up something at Plumas."

I caught them from the corner of my eye, mulling the words over, planning the words they wanted to say.

"My gear is all in the lockers," they said. "Maybe I can sell it so—"

"Absolutely not." I would seal their locker shut if I had to. "You are not selling anything, pet."

Definitely not when, by the looks of it, going to their uncle's place to pack up their stuff was not going to be an option. I was planning on running it by them, but if it had been, they would've already said something. They wouldn't have reacted so strongly, wouldn't have been so out of it for hours that their phone died and the only thing they could think of was alerting the security system in my gym. I didn't even remember talking about it in front of them, but it wasn't so out of the norm it would raise any flags.

Eli paid more attention to detail than people thought.

"Okay."

I'd thought they would put up more of a fight. I was glad they didn't, but I didn't love the resignation in their tone and their slouched body.

"We'll discuss more tomorrow," I said. "Abel is taking over at the gym so we can sort everything out."

3

ELI

"I know what I want."

After Erika had put me in a hoodie with what She said was the old logo of Her gym and a pair of joggers She had to roll so that I didn't drag the fabric all over Her floors, She'd moved us to the open concept living room. The couch was a sectional. It was soft—softer than I would've imagined—but even with its comfort, my courage to speak came from having my phone in my hands. It was still charging, but it somehow didn't get wet, and it worked.

Having my phone with me helped. It gave me another way to communicate if things got tough. I tried not to use it much, not to rely on it, but it was like having a safety blanket. It made things easier and less overwhelming.

Her clothes helped, too. They were warm, and the hoodie smelled like Her—like lemongrass and a hint of shea butter.

"Let's hear it, then."

I liked that, even though I knew She'd wanted to put me in bed, She'd dragged us here first. I wouldn't have relaxed fully without having evidence that my phone worked. It was old as fuck, and I should probably look into saving some money for a new one, but it was all I had.

Quite literally now.

Shit.

I blinked quickly. If I started crying again, or if I looked on the verge of it, Erika wouldn't say yes. It would go against everything She believed in, and She wasn't easily swayed once She'd made up Her mind about something. It was how I knew I could trust Her with anything. With everything.

"I want a contract." I put strength in my words, the conviction that had settled deep in my bones while my brain had whirled through everything and nothing all day. "With you."

"Eli..." Erika spoke slowly. "What are you talking about exactly?"

I swallowed.

She had to know.

There was no way She didn't. She just *had* to know.

"24/7. High protocol." I swallowed. "I need it, Mistress."

Erika shook Her head right away. It was my biggest fear coming to life. I scrambled, but there was nowhere to go.

"Eli, you're not in a place where we can negotiate that. You're too vulnerable right now."

My breath picked up speed. My chest heaved up and down. "I know what I want."

They were the same words I'd uttered before. They rolled familiarly down my tongue. I had to cling to them, had to make Her see.

"Eli..." Erika's tone grew sterner, sharper. More like the Mistress I knew. Strangely enough, even though I was still being rejected, even though it stung, I breathed easier. "Let's get you back on your feet first."

I shook my head.

I didn't want to get back on my feet.

I didn't know that I'd ever truly been on my feet, whatever that expression meant. Explaining it required too many words, too many thoughts pouring through my brain too fast for me to catch them.

I whimpered.

Erika shuffled closer. She wrapped Her hand around mine. "Text for your thoughts?"

My lips parted. That was María's line. María was a switch who played with me—and Erika—at the club sometimes, especially if Erika was on DM duty. I liked her. She was fun. We were just looking for different things.

But I knew Erika wasn't.

We were compatible. We wanted the same things, had the same core kinks.

"Eli?"

Shit.

Right. She'd used María's line because that was what María had started saying when she noticed I was struggling too much. It was her way of reminding me I could just write down what I needed to say. She said that getting the words out there was more important than how I got them out.

My eyes drifted down to the phone. I'd been clutching it between my hands. I probably looked silly, but Erika hadn't said anything. She called me out on many things, from my posture to the way I behaved around company, but She never said anything about my speech, or... anything else.

I glanced down. This wasn't the time to get lost in my thoughts, to drown inside my head. It wouldn't help my case, either. I needed Her to understand this wasn't a spur-of-the-moment decision. I wasn't saying things just because.

I never did that.

I never would.

i'm not asking because of my uncle, or my home

situation. Vanilla life has never made sense to me. i've told you before. And maybe it means i'm fucked in the head, but i don't think it does. Things make sense when i'm on my knees, or when i'm serving you, when the people around me have a set role, and i can think of them as subs, Littles, Domms, Sadists.

i don't want to figure out a job, or roommates, or an apartment. i want to be someone's slave.

No, i want to be your slave, Mistress Erika.

i know you. We've played on and off for years now, and i know we're compatible. i think you know, too. You have to know. And you know i let you know if i don't like something, or if i need something different. You've said i was good at that, that you wouldn't play with me if you hadn't made sure of it first.

i... i understand you're wary about the timing. i don't think i'd want to submit to you fully if you weren't, but... please, Mistress Erika.

My hand shook as I passed Her my phone. I didn't think that was my best writing. There was so much more I could've written, so many more things left unsaid.

It was too late now. I could only watch Her now, try to read Her expressions as She read through the lacking words. Reading Her was always challenging. Erika was amazing at putting up a strong front. There were little tells I'd begun to spot more easily, like the way She'd force Herself to sit straighter, or how She'd move Her hair off to Her back. It bothered Her when She was thinking hard about something and hair was touching Her face.

"You *are* good at setting your boundaries and safewording and asking for what you want." Erika nodded as She spoke the words, slowly, as if She was measuring every syllable. "That's not what I'm worried about."

"What…" I swallowed. "What then?"

My eyes smarted, stinging with more tears. I didn't know someone could cry so much in one day. I didn't like it. If I started crying again, Erika would for sure say no.

I needed Her to say yes.

"I'm worried that you would've never asked me this if today hadn't happened." Erika crossed Her arms over Her chest. "You've never expressed any interest in having anything outside of the club."

I frowned. That was… true, but it wasn't true for the reasons She thought.

It unsettled me that She might be wrong about something, as irrational as I knew the feeling to be. I understood why She'd have that impression, regardless.

"It's not…" I fidgeted with my hands. It would be easier to ask for my phone back, to just type the words. I might need to do it anyway, but I wanted to try. I had to try. "Belonging to you is all I've ever wanted. I dream about it. A lot."

"I didn't know you to be a flatterer."

I looked away. Heat crept up my cheeks. I wasn't flattering Her; I was just honest. I understood what She was saying, though.

"I couldn't ask for things outside of Plumas." I let out a shaky breath, shifting until I could bring my knees close to my chest. "It wasn't safe."

A part of me didn't want to look, but a bigger part of me couldn't fathom doing anything else. Erika squinted Her eyes. That was something else She did. She wasn't as obvious about it as Danny was, or even León, but I'd caught Her doing it a few times when She was putting pieces together in Her head. I loved watching Her, tracking every microexpression.

"Because of your uncle?"

More thoughts slapped me in the face, flashbacks about my family, about him standing up for me for reasons I didn't understand yet. He'd always been a complicated man, but I thought it would be all right if I didn't show the places where he could really hurt me.

"I thought…" I swallowed. "After I finished school. After I didn't depend on…"

I tried not to depend on him, and I covered most of my expenses. But I hadn't been ready to lose it all, to…

I screwed my eyes closed.

"You'd depend on me, with nothing to fall back on, Eli."

I winced. I was aware of it. The problem was, nothing sounded better than that.

But those weren't words I could say yet.

"I trust you." It was simple, but it was the most honest thing I could say. "And I… We can go slow. One rule at a time, even. Your pace."

If it were up to me, I'd dive deep into a full M/s dynamic, but I understood Erika's reticence. I had to respect it, to honor it.

I meant what I said. If She'd just jumped into it, hadn't taken a step back to assess this from every different angle, I wouldn't want Her.

Erika stood up from the couch. I didn't know what that meant, but my heart sped up as She added more distance between us. "Come with me."

"Yes, Mistress."

I never struggled less with words than when I was

agreeing to a command She gave. I didn't know what that said about me. I'd stopped seeing a speech therapist a few years back, when I turned eighteen, so it wasn't like I could ask. It was for the better, in a way. I couldn't imagine many speech therapists were versed in the world of kink.

Erika didn't wait. She didn't react to the honorific, either. She just turned around and began walking out of the living room area. I couldn't help but stare wistfully at the kitchen before following Her down the wide hallway. All the appliances were new. They still had that shiny polish to them. I knew Erika cooked because She was all about fresh ingredients and caring about what went in Her body. She must've renovated the space recently. I itched to run my finger over the marble, to open the fridge and start chopping the vegetables there.

It went beyond my love for cooking. It was about serving Her.

The thought would have to stay in my head for the time being.

Going too fast at Erika was not a good idea. She was the kind of Domme who wanted subs to speak their mind and rewarded them for it, but She was also the kind of Domme who needed to be ten steps ahead of someone. She couldn't be rushed there, either. She was the one holding the leash, directing people through those steps.

Erika turned on the light to the room past the bathroom I'd been in before. She gestured for me to walk inside. It was a bedroom, but it didn't look like Her room. The bed was that size which was bigger than a single but smaller than a double. It was tucked against the wall, too. There was nothing personal, just white and black accents.

"Get some sleep, pet. We'll talk tomorrow."

It stung. I curled my arms around my stomach. "B-but—"

Shit.

The word had slipped out before I realized what I was doing. I didn't want to be contrary. If Erika was telling me to sleep in a guest room, then that was what I had to do. Period.

"I'm upstairs if you need anything." It wasn't an invitation, but I clung to the words regardless. "We'll sit down and talk about this tomorrow after getting all the admin stuff done."

What admin stuff? Oh, the doctor and residence change. Erika and Abel had mentioned it while Abel drove us back to Erika's building. I still felt bad that he'd gone so out of his way for me. Maybe I could text Sergio tomorrow and make sure they understood how much it meant to me.

Texting with Sergio could take a lot out of me, but I still enjoyed it. He made me laugh every now and then, even though I was never supposed to when I was wearing my gimp suit.

"Thank you, Mistress."

Erika just gave me a curt nod.

In a movie, or one of the books Cece liked to secretly read and then talk about when they thought no one was listening, I would've spent all night tossing and turning. I was never a good sleeper. But the hoodie Erika had given me smelled of Her, and it was soft, and it *had* been a long shitty day.

4

ERIKA

"Are you going to be okay on your own?"

There was a time when doctors let a guest walk in, but they were becoming more and more strict. Personally, I found it infuriating. Most people who needed someone there for support had their motives. Either they struggled with anxiety when visiting a doctor's office, or they were too burned out by doctors who didn't listen to them and needed someone else to help them speak up.

"Yes." Eli pursed their lips as they shuffled in one of the plastic chairs in the waiting room. They were uncomfortable as fuck, but at least we'd arrived first thing in the morning, and we could find a bench of chairs without anyone there to make the space feel even more cramped. "Doctors can see my history."

I nodded. It still unnerved me, but I kept the thought to myself. Doctors, if they bothered to read Eli's file, could see about their delayed speech and history with therapy, but that didn't mean they had to be nice about it. Or maybe I was too burned out by my own experience with their treatment, and Eli had never had to deal with any of those biases.

I wouldn't know.

A nurse came out of one of the doctor's offices. She'd drawn my blood a couple of times. She was nicer than most, but there wasn't a lot more I could say about her.

"Eli García?"

She didn't deadname Eli, either. They'd had their name officially changed, and doctors' offices didn't require any official documents to add one's chosen name anyway, but it wouldn't be the first time doctors ignored it.

Eli exchanged a quick look with me before they stood up and followed the nurse into the office.

I hated it, but I sank down in the chair the second they were out of view.

I fished my phone out of my jacket one second later.

There were always texts and notifications in the club's app to take care of.

ABEL

How's Eli?

ERIKA

Easy, Papa Bear.

They've just walked into the doctor's office.

ABEL

No fever?

ERIKA

No, they seem fine.

Still shell-shocked, to a degree, but I'd stuffed a thermometer under their armpit, and it came out okay. I only gave them an aspirin after they begrudgingly admitted to having a headache.

JUST ONE RULE

ERIKA

> How's the gym?

> I could probably sneak in a couple of hours if it gets too crowded.

> Or take Eli with me. They can help in the reception.

ABEL

> ... Please tell me you're not hiring them.

I locked the screen the second the text arrived. It was all I could do not to groan in frustration. Mónica and Abel—and their Littles—seemed to think it was hilarious to tease me about my way of fixing people's problems by offering them a job at the gym.

It had only happened twice, and only one of them had taken me up on the offer.

Most importantly, though, it wasn't about being the control freak they said I was. Well, I had tendencies that aligned with those of a control freak, but offering people who were close to me a job when they needed that financial independence—or a way to leave a shitty situation of their own making—wasn't about that. It was about community. If I had the resources to help my community, I was going to use them.

I didn't just talk the talk. I walked it, too, and the truth was, in today's society, I could offer a shoulder to cry on all I wanted, but that shoulder wasn't going to make as big a difference as material resources—jobs, money, a place to stay.

Besides, I still needed a receptionist since it was clearer and clearer that Kara wasn't leaving Mónica's construction company.

Then again, Eli would need to pick up the phone. I didn't care about the people who showed up and might go to them to ask about a class or struggled with the turnstile. Those could wait Eli out, or Eli could write something and they could read. The phone would probably be trickier.

It didn't ring that often. I supposed Abel and I could still answer it like we'd been doing so far, but... That wouldn't be fair, either. There was a difference between offering someone a job because I could and I knew they were qualified to do it and offering it as a sort of... beneficence.

I didn't do beneficence.

There was a lot to talk about when we went back to the duplex.

IT HAD BEEN A PRODUCTIVE MORNING, I supposed. I needed a session at the boxing ring with Abel or whoever would be available and willing to let me burn through all the noise in my head. Everything had worked out, though. Eli got a new prescription, and they liked their new doctor. The pharmacist didn't make much of a fuss, either, and the people at the bank didn't bat an eye when we gave them my address to send new cards to.

Giving them my address didn't mean I was on board with just jumping into a 24/7 dynamic, but regardless of what happened there, Eli needed new cards if going to retrieve the current ones from their uncle's place was not an option.

Apparently, Eli's phone was too old to carry their cards, so they just had the cash the bank had let them withdraw while we were there.

No way I was letting them use it until everything was sorted. Between the club and the gym, I didn't struggle with money. It didn't make a difference if I had to take care of Eli financially for the next couple of weeks—or months.

Besides, if they were serious about a full-blown 24/7 dynamic, the kind I really wanted? Yeah, that meant they weren't spending their own money.

"Mistress?"

Fuck.

I'd been staring at the coffee machine for too long. I'd come here with a purpose, dammit.

I pulled out my phone and opened the app I used for my grocery lists. There was an option to collaborate, but I didn't know if Eli's phone carried the app or if they had the storage.

My phone would do for now.

"If you want to be my slave, you're in charge of the kitchen. Both cooking and keeping the fridge and pantry stocked." I slid the phone with the opened app toward them. "Write down anything and everything you need for the week, and I'll buy it tomorrow."

It was more brazen than it should've been. I never would've started a discussion of TPE and M/s dynamics with a sub like this, but Eli wasn't just any sub. I knew them, and no matter how much the timing was... questionable, they'd been right last night. Eli out of kink made no sense. They did all right, but it wasn't a space they could settle down in easily. And I'd known them for years. Everyone around us talked about how it made no sense that we were casual.

They were right. It didn't make sense.

There had just always been something else going on. I was getting the gym off the ground, and the club, and then I was transitioning out of sex work to focus fully on the two, and then we had new people who needed more overseeing.

I had refused to even hint at starting something more serious when I couldn't give it my one hundred percent.

Eli took the phone between their hands as if it was a treasure that could break if they weren't careful. "Yes, Mistress. Thank you."

I hummed. "What do you want out of a 24/7 dynamic, Eli, other than being in a sub headspace?"

"I want to..." Eli chewed on their lip. I didn't think it had anything to do with voicing the words out loud, and everything to do with regular nerves. "I want to serve, but... Ultimately? My deepest fantasy is to be an object you own."

I nodded. It wasn't something they hadn't hinted at before in our scenes, or something they hadn't written about in the app.

"What does an object do?"

I moved closer, standing between the stool they'd sat on and the kitchen island. Ideally, right about now I'd be telling them to kneel, but Abel and I had both noted the bruises forming and scratched skin last night.

I had no doubt they'd do it if I asked, no hesitation. Maybe if the reason behind the scratches was different, I'd taunt them with it, but not today.

"It..." Eli licked their bottom lip. "It exists as Mistress's property, for her pleasure. It has no will of its own, doesn't think, doesn't act. It doesn't do anything Mistress doesn't expressly ask, outside of its chores." A pause. My heart thundered in my chest, probably the same way Eli's was. "It relegates everything to Mistress. Becomes an empty vessel for her to mold."

I clenched my thighs. Fuck, I was the one supposed to keep it together, but Eli was pushing all the right buttons. It was luck, and probably years of experience handling brats that knew how to push buttons in a different way, that gave me the control to only raise their chin with two fingers.

A shiver raced down their spine.

"Do you want me to use it/its pronouns when talking or thinking about you, Eli?"

It didn't escape my notice that was what Eli had been doing.

"Yes, Mistress." The words came out in a rushed whimper, more high-pitched than *its* voice usually went.

"Do you want to update your info in the club's app?"

I could update it, technically, but it should come from Eli.

Eli nodded before moving forward. My breath puffed against its cheek. Its lips parted.

Fuck. I was getting too wet, and we hadn't gone over half of the things I'd set out to cover. I didn't want to take a step back, but I was supposed to be the voice of reason, the Domme with the steel-clad morals.

It wasn't an option.

"Yes, Mistress."

"Okay." I cleared my throat and closed my eyes for a second. Maybe two seconds. "Does an object follow commands, cues?"

"Yes, Mistress."

Inhale. Exhale. That was all I had to focus on.

"What does an object do outside or at Plumas?"

The answer didn't come right away this time. Eli took its time. Fuck, I so wanted to lean into humiliation, to tease about why an object would take long to answer.

It wasn't the time nor the place, but the desire was still there, burning through me.

People thought that because I appeared collected and in control, that I was unaffected.

It couldn't be further from the truth.

"It's still Mistress's property. In the club, it does what Mistress says. Outside, it represents Mistress. Makes her proud."

I traced my hand down Eli's neck, its shoulder, its arm. There should be some adjustment period, some struggle to get used to the new pronouns, to everything that was coming out of its mouth.

There wasn't any.

Nothing had felt more natural, more right.

"What if Mistress wanted to hang a cardboard sign that said Free Use around the object's neck and left the room?"

It was one of the deepest fantasies I hadn't shared with anyone. It seemed out of reach, something that needed too many previous steps to ever be doable.

If this thing worked out with Eli…

I could feel the heat between my legs building up, the pressure there growing. It took all my focus not to tremble with need, throw caution to the wind, and force Eli's mouth around my clit. My new object would oblige happily—would thank me afterward even.

"Th-the object would let everyone in the room use it. It would do it proudly."

My fingers clenched, curling around Eli's thigh. I needed to put myself together, stat.

"What if Mistress was sick, or Dropped?"

Eli's half-hooded gaze widened. Its breath hitched. I followed the way its throat bobbed up and down two, three times.

"It would take care of you, Mistress. Reach out to others. Object is there to bring Mistress release, and calm, and…" Eli paused, lips parted. "Everything Mistress needs."

I nodded. It was a good answer. I believed Eli, too, but I could also see the creases in its forehead. I'd noted the way it stammered before. Eli might do better verbally when it was the two of us alone, but being verbal the entire time took a toll. It had exhausted my now slave.

Well, not yet slave.

I kept moving ten steps ahead, and not in the way that ensured things went smoothly.

"Being in a high protocol, 24/7 dynamic with me isn't just about sex. I mentioned the cooking and grocery lists already."

"I understand, Mistress."

"Don't talk," I said. "Just nod or use your phone if you have something to say."

Confusion marred Eli's features for a second before relief washed all over its body. Those creases began fading as I ran my fingers through them, too.

An exhale left its lips.

"It's not about becoming my maid, either, or losing all your agency. As deep as we can go into a fantasy, that's not realistic or safe for either of us," I said. Talking helped reel in some of that urgency threatening to overtake me and clear my head enough to get us back on track. "If you become my slave, my object or whatever you want to call it, you need safeguards. You need to accept routines that are about taking you out of the object mindset."

Eli furrowed its brow, its lips twisting to the side.

The gesture was almost sweet.

"You can't spend 24/7 with me here, or even at the club. I'll want you to go out with other subs and to take up one activity that has nothing to do with kink." Eli didn't react when I mentioned the subs, but it whimpered when I added the last part. I'd counted on it. I barreled through before I pointed to its phone. "I want you to journal, and I want access to that journal. You'll have access to mine, too. And I want a word that means Eli the Object leaves, and I get the person instead."

It wasn't all, but those were the main points. They were things I'd learned from trying to settle down with other subs that ultimately didn't work. It was easy to just say the chemistry wasn't there or we just weren't a good fit, but that didn't seem responsible when so much was at stake.

A relationship based around a Total Power Exchange, or anything close to it, wasn't as quote-unquote simple as negotiating a spanking. It was more psychological, went deeper than sending someone into subspace with a paddle or a flogger. There were finances, and jobs, and degrees of autonomy to keep in consideration.

Eli shuffled on the stool. It didn't look me in the eye, but its fingers curled around my wrists. A whimper left its lips.

I wasn't one for sweet gestures or traditional displays of affection, but I kissed its forehead before I dug its phone out of the clothes it borrowed from me.

Eli grabbed it right away, unlocking it and opening the Notes app it used.

> *i want to negotiate the activity. i accept everything else, and i understand why it would be important for most slaves, Mistress Erika, but i want this because i don't want anything to do with the vanilla world. i've tried to fit in it for years. it doesn't work. i don't want to keep trying*
>
> *this is about getting rid of stress for me, and a vanilla activity would put that stress back on my shoulders*

How could people type so fast?

Well, I supposed for Eli it made sense. They relied on it to communicate with others, but damn, it would be nice if there were more people like León, who got teased for being a slow typer and would rather call instead.

"Okay, I hear what you're saying." I took a deep breath. I heard what Eli was saying; it made sense to the point that I felt responsible for not predicting it. There would be time for beating myself over it later. For now, my mind whirled with possibilities and alternatives. I understood Eli's point, but they needed somewhere, something that gave them power. It was even trickier because they had no family and no friends that weren't fellow kinksters as far as I knew. They'd once mentioned they related to Sergio's feelings when it came to being bullied, but I hadn't been able to dig in deeper. "What about having more responsibility at the club, for starters? We'd reassess every once in a while, too."

Eli's head cocked to its side. It didn't speak, but it mouthed a very clear *how*.

Its note about not wanting anything to do with the vanilla life meant my half-assed consideration that it could come to work at the gym was out. But Eli could technically work at the club. It would take weight off my plate, which was something it wanted, and it would give Eli more power.

"Be in charge of the app."

The more I thought about it, the more sense it made. Some people came straight to me or one of the other founders when they wanted to join, but more and more, people joined in through the app, and they requested to become members from there. I liked that it made the process more accessible for some, but having to scan through all their activity there was a pain in the ass. And we needed moderators. With more people who only stuck to online interactions, it meant there was more danger for the members who were actually part of the community.

It might not be as perfect as having to interact face-to-face with people from a position of more power, but it would elevate Eli in the eyes of the people who were already members. Eli wouldn't just be the club's objectification slut or my slave. It would be the app's moderator, too. It would have power over the online newcomers and a tie to the community in more general terms.

Eli nodded along as I explained my thought process. It had no questions or suggestions to renegotiate.

"Last thing is money and chores," I said.

Eli pulled back, teeth gnawing at its lip. There was no way I'd let that go if we went along with this.

"Cooking," Eli whispered.

"Yes." I didn't think whispering or speaking out loud made a lot of difference, but I supposed I could be more lenient today. "I want you to cook and to manage the kitchen, but as I said, it's not about becoming my maid. If you hadn't gone to culinary school and wanted to be a home chef, I wouldn't even suggest it."

Eli's eyes sparked with something that looked like joy. I ignored the fact that my chest tightened. "A cleaning person drops by for a couple of hours on Thursdays. You don't have to worry about keeping the place spotless, but I will not accept any disrespect toward them, and it is not an excuse to let things become a mess."

I just hired a cleaning company because between managing the gym and the club, there weren't enough hours in the day.

Eli nodded, its expression turning more serious.

"I pay them on a monthly basis, so you don't have to do anything other than look decent while they're here." It was an attempt of a joke. Eli's lips tilted up into the start of a grin. I never claimed to be particularly funny, but I could try. "As for money, you are not to contribute anything if you're living here as mine. You can keep your website if you want or not, that's your choice, but you contribute with your labor. Is that clear?"

Eli raised a hand before unlocking its phone again.

I waited as its fingers slid across the keyboard on the screen.

> *if you think about it, it's a bit ridiculous to think that an object would have to pay anything*
> *i'm comfortable with that, Mistress*
> *i think i would like to keep my website up, but it's not just about the money. i like... the objectification that borders on dehumanization that comes from some of the comments. and i think i'll like it even more if i'm yours, and maybe we can play with it?*

I hummed. "I haven't forgotten you're a slut for humiliation, don't worry."

Eli moaned as its head bobbed up and down, lip trapped between its teeth. Eli wasn't the only one in need of release.

"I'd love to read you all the filthy comments men leave in your posts, how they see you as just a disgusting set of holes to break and throw away after." I moved my hand back to Eli's jaw, tightening my grip there. Eli's nostrils flared before its gaze hooded. "But there is more we have to talk about."

"What else?" The moan that accompanied the words was so pitiful, I almost felt bad.

I didn't show it. "This is the second time you disobey, Eli. I told you not to speak, didn't I?"

Its eyes widened, golden brown spheres staring at me, searching my face. A tremor ran through its body.

"It's okay. Today." I cleared my throat. "The other thing is, I don't want you to use your money while you're here, not without discussing it with either me or another Domm. Down the line, I'll grant you access to my bank accounts and you won't need permission to use them, but in the meantime, I want you to ask me whenever you need money. I don't care if it's because you're joining Kara and Sergio for their milkshake dates or if it's because you want new gear."

Two seconds passed, then Eli nodded.

I didn't think Eli was bad at handling their financials, but this was what I meant with safeguards. If something happened, or if things went south between us, even if Eli could use the app or its time as a home chef with me as experience, I wanted it to have the biggest cushion possible.

"Good." Fuck, Eli was gorgeous, and it wasn't even doing any of the things that turned me on. "Now follow me to my room, slut."

I was rushing, going through some things way sooner than I would with anyone else. It was Eli, though. I had to believe the years we'd played together, all the times I'd watched Eli like a hawk while María acted in charge of group play at Plumas, counted for something.

5

ELI

I didn't know how to stay in my body—how to follow Erika down the hallway without exploding. I did, though. Everything was coming true.

I was brimming with energy, with relief, with desire. Everything mingled together in my head. I didn't know where one emotion started and where it ended. It didn't matter.

Erika's room was more like what I'd imagined it would be. A large bed was in the middle, with a thick, fluffy-looking mattress covered by a grey duvet. Silk, probably. There was an armchair next to a tall window. I could see Erika sitting there, writing down observations on subs or ideas for pain sessions. She always had the best ideas to make a sub cry.

The wooden furniture was a lighter grey than the bed. There wasn't a lot, but there were some shelves full of photographs, and a couple of drawings hung in frames.

I wanted to take in everything in the room, but my eyes kept snapping back to the two drawings. They were breathtaking. I didn't know enough about art to talk about the technique, or even the material. All I knew was that they encapsulated everything about Erika that had brought me here.

"I got those commissioned after I paid off my mortgage," Erika said. I whipped my head around, but She didn't seem upset my attention had drifted. Some Owners could get upset over such things. I'd known Erika long enough to know She wasn't one of them, but it was never a bad idea to double-check. "They're from a shoot I made back when I was working as a pro Domme."

I knew about that. It was in Erika's profile in the app, but it was also something She was never shy discussing. It was why I turned to Her when I first thought about starting a spicy website. My goal had never been to make millions through it, but I'd wanted something to give me more... independence.

She was beautiful. I wanted to say the words, to praise the artist who had worked on the two drawings. I'd already disobeyed twice, though, as She'd pointed out. Other D-types —Daddies and brat tamers—might enjoy the cheekiness of me doing it, but Erika was not that type of Domme. I didn't want Her to be. I just wanted Her to make everything go quiet.

The drawings were framed one next to the other. The one to the right depicted Erika's profile. She was in a black rubber suit, Her hair out of Her face in a high ponytail, and a single tail whip in Her hands. The next drawing showed Her back, the glistening of the rubber, the movement in Her goddess braids. There was so much movement in both paintings.

I could worship them forever and die happy. I kept the silly thought to myself.

"Do you want to get on the bed for me? Lose the pants, too."

Yes, Mistress.

I nodded, remembering not to speak out loud. After taking the pair of joggers off, I folded them and placed them on top of the nightstand closest to me.

The mattress was as fluffy as I'd thought it would feel, the material sinking under my weight as I kneeled on the center of it. Erika hadn't said how She wanted me, so I didn't know how to kneel or present myself. I went on instinct when I positioned myself so that my knees were spread apart, palms digging into my thighs. I took inventory of the rest of my body—it was important to keep a straight spine, to square up my shoulders, keep my chin up but my gaze down. Erika liked to see the strength in a sub's body.

"I left out discussing anything that has to do with the sexual aspects of this because I think we're both well versed on each other's body by now."

I swallowed, then nodded. She was right, of course. She played my body like a fiddle—had done it for years now. There was no one I trusted more with it than Her.

I knew Her body, too. I knew how She liked to get off, to be touched, to be licked. I knew the sounds to make, the things that brought Her the most pleasure. It was my job as Her slut.

Erika took my hands in Hers. She pushed me back, shifted me around until I was on my back. "Remind me how you use your words when you can't use your words in a scene."

My lips parted, but I obeyed. I knew what She was talking about. One squeeze meant green. Two squeezes meant yellow. Three squeezes meant red. Sometimes She added more commands, but I didn't need more than those three to get my point across.

Erika's eyes glinted with approval as I demonstrated. Warmth spread through my core.

"Good." Erika only needed one hand to trap mine

together. She used the other to trace my figure, the curves of my body. It didn't matter that there were clothes still covering me. It didn't take away from the intimacy of the touch. "I've been so turned on since you started speaking, I should be ashamed of myself."

I shook my head.

I didn't know how to convey it, but I didn't want Her to feel shame. I wanted Her words to wash over me, the knowledge that I had such an effect on Her. It felt right and wrong. A selfish part of me preened at the fact that I held such power. The part of me that wanted to sink into this dynamic scoffed at the selfish part. I was no one to hold that power. It wasn't my place to hold it.

My thighs clenched. I could feel the wetness building up, threatening to dribble down my thighs. Sometimes I felt like lust caused such a big reaction in me, I'd become a fountain. It was a fantasy, too, to have everyone drink off my groin until I dried up, only I never did.

Mockery was involved in that fantasy, too. The hot tendrils of humiliation curled around my limbs, sucking me in.

Erika let out a guttural groan. She hadn't touched me yet, but my hips lifted off the mattress regardless.

"You really are meant to be the perfect slut, aren't you?"

One squeeze. *Yes, Mistress.*

I tried to stay quiet, but a whimper slipped past my lips. Heat crept up my cheeks. I knew better than this. I could stay quiet and take everything Erika gave me.

Erika didn't say anything. I supposed She was pacing Herself, even if I personally thought there was no need for it. But this was about me not thinking, not holding the reins or making choices.

"Do you remember the first time you volunteered as my slut for a workshop?"

Green. I could never forget that day. I'd been so nervous, the anticipation making me jittery even now, years later. Once I'd been face-to-face with Her, however, all the nerves had dissipated. Only She had existed, the strength She exuded. I never told Her, but that was the moment I knew belonging to Her, completely, would be the only thing that made sense.

"You said you needed to come at least twice a day, that you were addicted to it and loved the embarrassment that came with it." Erika hummed. I nodded. I couldn't tear my eyes off Her, even though it would probably make things easier. "I told you I was more interested in making my subs suffer than I was in getting them off."

My toes curled. I had no idea how She still had this effect on me. She was only talking, and I felt on the edge of a cliff, too afraid to take a step forward but refusing to take a step back or crawl to safety.

"Do you still get yourself off every day?"

One squeeze. Erika's nostrils flared. Her pupils widened, darkening Her gaze further.

"If an object only does what its Mistress says explicitly, does that mean you only come if I tell you to?"

Yes, Mistress. One squeeze. I bit my lip, hard, before I let out another sound. It didn't matter that She was more lenient with me today. I had to—I wanted to—prove myself, to let Her know I'd be up to the challenge, even without Her asking me to.

It was my sole purpose. Well... It was what I wanted to have as my sole purpose. I was still waiting for Erika to pronounce Herself, to state that we were doing this, that I was worthy of it. Of Her.

"I want you to update the list you gave me of what you consider real punishments," Erika said. She kept going back and forth between being consumed by desire and the seriousness with which She addressed all things kink. It should put me off, make me dizzy. I just craved more of it. "But right now, I want to put you to the test."

One squeeze. *Yes, Mistress.* I'd do anything; I'd chase any release She might grant me.

Erika chuckled. It was a dark sound, but it wasn't one that scared me, even if my heart beat faster as I watched Her lean forward. Her body hovered over me before She slid off the bed, moving to one of the drawers.

"I am getting you off like you say you need," Erika drawled. I couldn't see what She was getting, but I knew enough to wait for the other shoe to drop, for the addition that would make this a test and would circle back to Erika's trip down memory lane. "But you are going to be quiet while I do it."

The challenge in the command was made clear when She turned around, brandishing a Hitachi wand. The strongest European model. There was one like it in the club, too. I'd only seen it in porn videos before the first time Erika used it on me. When the vibrating head had pressed against my clit, I'd screamed so loud, I was still mortified by it.

My mouth dried up. Could I do it?

That first time, Erika had made Her mocking displeasure clear. She'd kept me gagged at the club for the next five days I was in attendance. When anybody asked, She just offered them the toy to use on me. It had been one of the most intense things.

She'd used it more times after that, but I'd always been gagged, and I'd always been loud regardless.

"Well?" Erika raised an eyebrow when She reached me. Her fingers intertwined with mine before I could wonder how She wanted me to respond. "Playing with me in a TPE dynamic won't look the same as playing at Plumas. I'm going to demand more of you. Same as how you demand more of me."

I screwed my eyes closed. I didn't like how that sounded. I wanted to protest, to say I was no one to demand anything of Her, but that was the part where fantasy crashed with reality. I *was* demanding more of Her—the responsibility of handling my entire life, of holding all that power over my head.

I squeezed Her hand, once.

I would prove that I'd give Her anything She demanded.

A small smile grazed Her lips. I liked the feeling that I'd put it there, but the reinforcement that came from it didn't calm my racing heart. It didn't get rid of the fear that I was not going to make it, that I was going to let Her down.

Erika turned on the wand after plugging it into the charger by Her nightstand. I heard the buzzing as She upped the settings. She never started on the lowest setting. All I could do was follow the white head of the toy as it leered closer and closer. The buzzing grew stronger, the head moving with it, sending pulses in a punishing rhythm that undid me every time.

There was no warning. She squeezed my hand, but I didn't know if that was a reminder meant for me or Herself. It didn't matter. I had yet to look away from the toy. I was too aware of where it was, how close it was.

My underwear was gone quickly. There was no fanfare, no delaying or making a big thing out of it.

The moment the head touched my skin, it was like a current zapped through my body. All my muscles tensed up as if I was hit by a live wire. My jaw dropped open, my mouth frozen in a silent O. I buckled, lifting off the bed. Erika held me close. There was something in Her gaze, but following any train of thought was impossible. I couldn't dissect anything, couldn't read into anything.

Somehow, I didn't make a sound, but inside, everything was screaming. It was too much, too hard. I screwed my eyes closed. There was too much stimuli. I couldn't take it. My heart thundered so loud against my ribs, it rivaled the loudness of the wand buzzing. I clenched my jaw shut, biting on the inside of my cheek. I breathed through my nose heavily, too rapidly. I knew I had to calm down, but I couldn't.

My clit throbbed under the punishing ministrations of the toy. My eyes pooled with tears, but these weren't ones I minded shedding. I clenched my fists—one around the silky duvet, another around Erika's wrist. I huffed, then panicked. Was that considered a noise?

I didn't have time to get lost in the panic. The settings in the wand were upped again. I convulsed through it. When I couldn't scream, everything was much more intense. I'd read something about it once in a post by a slave in the kind of dynamic I wanted to achieve.

Reading hadn't prepared me for the onslaught of sensation, need, and fear. I had no control over my body while I'd never fought to be more in control.

I still made no sound. I still replayed Erika's words in my head. Over and over, until they made no sense.

"You look perfect like this," Erika said, Her voice piercing through the fog in my brain. Silent sobs racked my body, bursts of tears that made my lips wobble streaming down my cheeks. She made a humming sound. "Mine to keep crying and suffering for as long as I want. Isn't that right?"

One squeeze. It was painful to get my tense, clenched up muscles to cooperate. It didn't matter.

It shocked Her that I responded—that I had the wits to do it. I knew because She paused, the pressure of the wand not as hard for a second. I didn't know if it gave me a respite or if it was something else to cry about. I didn't have time to decide, the toy soon back where it belonged.

The slight switch in pressure had me buckling wildly, my entire body rigid and on the edge of complete collapse. I didn't want to move away, but my hips rolled of their own accord. Erika followed the erratic movements easily enough.

More tears fell, more silent sobs that felt louder than anything I'd experienced before.

I came.

It wasn't like any other orgasm. I couldn't bathe in the aftermath. It was just a rush of endorphins that unclenched my muscles only for rigidness to set in once again the second more vibrations came.

I kicked my legs against the duvet. A voice at the back of my head said good sluts didn't kick around, didn't cause a scene. I'd beg Erika to train me better later. She hadn't said anything about staying still, even though I knew She cared about those things.

She'd just asked me to be quiet.

I was quiet.

Somehow.

Everything was too still, too loud, too fast, too slow. All sensations zapped through my body with too much force and intensity. I couldn't catalog them all. Everything throbbed and felt numb at the same time.

"I can see how hard you're working to keep quiet," Erika said. There was mockery in Her voice. I stifled a hiccup. She chuckled. My stomach churned for a second, but She didn't put a stop to anything. I opened my eyes to check, even if my sight was blurred at the edges because too many tears pooled there. Erika just looked down at me. She pressed the head of the wand harder. I wanted to scream so fucking badly, but I didn't know if I even remembered how to make a sound. "You're so desperate to please me, aren't you? So desperate for me to strip everything away."

More convulsions followed. I didn't keep track of what it

was my body did exactly. I just let my second orgasm rush through me, the wave of endorphins staying a bit longer this time. They left me on a cloud, away from everything and everyone.

I closed my eyes again. Or maybe everything just went black of its own volition.

I didn't know.

It didn't matter.

Things were quiet when I opened my eyes next.

There was no buzzing, no toy. A whimper broke its way past my lips.

Erika lay down next to me. She held me. She pressed her lips against the crown of my head.

I tried to take stock of my body. My clit throbbed, oversensitive in that way that left the skin feeling too soft.

"You've made me so proud, slut."

Those words tore at the dams I hadn't realized I'd built.

I cried, sobbed, screamed. I couldn't exactly tell why. A mix of everything, probably—the events of yesterday I hadn't fully processed, Erika, the scene.

She held me, shifted me so I was on top of Her. She told me to let it all out, said She was here, I was okay now. She said I made Her proud again.

I didn't know how long I stayed there, how many times She had to say the same words, caressing my back in a soothing manner I would've never associated with Her. Then again, I'd never lost it around Her like this.

My chin quivered as I looked up at Her. I swiped at my cheeks. I didn't like crying when it wasn't for a Domm's pleasure—when I hadn't consented to it. At least I managed to put a stop to them now.

Kind of.

Erika tilted my head up. "Are you feeling better?"

JUST ONE RULE

I cleared my throat. My vocal cords felt jarred, dusty. "Dehydrated."

"Wait here." I'd barely said the word, and Erika was moving, jumping out of the bed.

A part of me felt the absence, mourned it, wanted to spill more tears and whimper because I didn't want Her to leave me. Another part felt warm, cozy in the knowledge that Erika took good care of me. She always did.

She was back seconds later. It wasn't enough time to miss Her. I sat up when She entered the room again, thanked Her when She handed me a tall glass of water.

It was cold, but not the kind of cold that would freeze my synapses. I hadn't expected anything different—I'd explained once how I liked my water—but I was in that headspace where everything felt more special and touching.

"May I ask a question, Mistress?"

Erika's lips tilted upward. I was one of the few people who actually addressed Her in the high protocol way She liked. It had just always made sense to me. Secretly, I thought it was disrespectful for the other subs not to address Her properly while in the club, outside of using an honorific, but I knew that was wrong of me. No Domm was owed any special treatment.

"You may."

Right.

I had a question. "Could we have a trial period?"

Erika frowned. I had Her rapt attention on me right away. "What do you mean?"

I swallowed. I supposed the question hadn't been as self-explanatory as I'd hoped. "I know it's important to move slow. But can we have a… week… where we go full out? I think I need to experience that."

There were two reasons. Three, really. One, I was the kind

of person who preferred jumping in a cold pool to slowly sliding in until my body got used to the water. Two, I didn't know if it was a result of my entire foundation being rocked the way it had been, but I needed that connection, that intensity—a taste, at the very least. Three, and this might be the most sensible reason... I'd never actually been in a TPE dynamic. I'd only fantasized about them while harboring a crush on Her. Erika mentioned changes in all areas—She'd already given me a taste, right here. But I needed to see. I needed the proof that I wasn't just clinging to the first thing in front of me, that I needed all the new changes and rules Erika wanted to give me.

"No."

Wait. "No?"

I frowned.

Why?

Erika didn't look like She was teasing, or like that *no* was part of a game. "Simple. I'm already moving faster with you than I would with any other sub. And you've already gotten tiny trial periods every time you've scened with me at the club."

"It doesn't feel the same." I managed to get the words out.

There was less tension in my body after a scene that felt heavier for one reason or another. Less tension made speaking easier.

"It isn't," She agreed. "But you're going to have to trust me on this one."

I did.

I trusted Her.

Trusting Her was why I was here in the first place.

"Yes, Mistress. Please, may I ask you to forgive me?"

Erika chuckled. "I'll think of something so you can make up for it later. Now you can drink your water, then make me come after you're done."

The air caught at the back of my throat. "Yes, Mistress."

I thought of making Her come as a privilege. It wasn't something that happened every time we played. Most of the time, scenes with Erika meant that She'd play with my body, make me beg—or hope I could beg—and then She'd rub Herself until She came. I wondered if making Her come was one of Her new demands for me. It felt wrong to ask. I wasn't supposed to be greedy.

It was a balancing act, asking Her for what I wanted, all while wanting to be little more than a toy for Her to use.

6

ERIKA

I accepted the towel from Abel without question. I'd just had two kickboxing classes back-to-back because the temporary trainer who led the second class had canceled last minute. When I saw the schedule on the computer, I'd welcomed it.

There was a chance I'd shot too close to the sun.

"Save it."

Abel looked like he was dying to hit me with an *I told you so*. I was not having it.

He just shook his head, grinning stupidly. Sergio was rubbing off on too many people. I wouldn't change anything about the bratty boy, but it would be nice to remind people that reverence was a fucking thing.

"How's Eli doing? Sergio said something about pronouns on the app, but I don't know if they're texting."

I rolled my eyes. "I thought by now you'd know. If it moves, your boy's texting it."

The well-natured jab put a sappy smile on my old friend's face. I had to say, it took some getting used to, but damn. I'd missed seeing him like this. He'd been burned out and struggling for far too long.

"Fair enough. But Eli's staying with you, right?"

"Yes."

I hadn't texted the group chat about any of it yet. For one, it had just happened, and unlike others, I wasn't glued to the device. For another, I still wanted Mónica to look into the apartments, and I still wanted to let Eli settle in my duplex, see if it felt the same way after there was more time to process.

Abel had more questions. I knew it, and I wasn't running from them, but I spotted a guy about to use one of the weight machines without a spotter.

He'd pretend the banners all over the machines were not big enough.

"Hey, there." I walked to him, Abel standing where he was. Crowding someone only made a confrontation more likely. I didn't recognize the man, but that wasn't too surprising. More and more people were signing up from the website, and Abel had started signing them up, too. It was good for my bank account, but I missed the days when I was lifting this place off the ground and I actually knew everyone who walked in. "Please remember to ask one of the staff or another gym member to spot you if you're going to use the machines."

It was bothersome at times, but I'd rather have that than an accident.

The man had the decency to blush. It wouldn't be the first time they tried posturing about their macho jizz. If only they knew I'd been paid for years to humiliate that reflex out of them. "Right. Sorry. Abel mentioned it when he showed me around the gym, but… Habit."

That was fair enough. "No problem. I'm Erika. Want me to spot you?"

"Yeah. Thanks."

It was only me and Abel on the floor right now. I really didn't want to avoid him, but rules were rules.

THE HOUSE SMELLED divine when I walked in. I let the smells waft all over me before slipping out of my sneakers and hanging my coat on the rack at the entrance.

Eli had asked if it was to come greet me when I got home. I said a tentative yes, unless it was cooking or doing anything else I'd asked of it. The answer pacified it.

I worried that Eli was sinking into the role too fast, but... trust went both ways. I reminded myself that if Eli wasn't safe to play, I wouldn't have been doing it for years now. It would've raised some flags—if not in me, in any of the friends who'd witnessed our interactions.

All my friends said was I needed to take my head out of my ass. Kara said it more nicely—she just said she shipped us together.

I didn't mind telling Abel or Mónica, but I was not looking forward to the ruckus the Littles and brats would make out of it.

María was someone else to keep in mind here.

All that would have to wait.

Stepping into the living area, I saw Eli checking over a pot. There were timers I didn't remember I owned and chopping boards all over the counter.

Note to self: Eli was not a clean cook, nor were they one of those who insisted on clearing a station before moving to the next step.

"I'm making miso soup, with a side of vegetable tempura

to use some of the fresh produce you had in the fridge, Mistress."

I hummed. I'd driven earlier in the morning to get the groceries Eli had written down in the app, but I was glad being a messy cook didn't translate into being a wasteful one.

"It smells good, pet."

"Thank you, Mistress."

I settled on watching Eli for now. Yesterday had been more of a roller coaster than I'd anticipated—for the both of us, but Eli was the one in a more vulnerable position here.

"It'll all be ready in five, Mistress Erika."

"Good." I massaged a knot on my shoulder as I spoke. "Abel asked about you. Sergio has questions about your update in the app."

The start of a chuckle caught at the back of Eli's throat. "He texted. Wants to meet up."

I sat straighter. "What did you say?"

Eli shrugged before grabbing a tray and two bowls from the cupboards above the counter. "I'll drop by his place tomorrow while you're at work."

There was no bite to the words, no resentment. I'd worried that Eli would not take nicely to my suggestion—that wasn't really a suggestion—of meeting up with subs more often. The slut seemed content, though. Relaxed, even if this was its first official day as my slave.

"How do you feel about doing that?" I pressed anyway.

Eli used a ladle to pour the soup in the bowls. "I'm a bit nervous. I've only been around Sergio at the club or during brunch."

I nodded. That made sense. Sergio was the social butterfly who tended to lure everyone for an outing. He was our main recruiter for the club, too, but Eli had always been hard to track down.

"If he's asked to meet up at his place, he'll most likely be wearing diapers and acting the same as he does for the play-dates at the club."

Eli didn't go to those—those events were strictly about age play, and nothing about coloring and snuggling with stuffies interested the slut—but it was there when the play-dates ended. That was enough.

"That's okay with me." Eli bobbed its head up and down, as if having a conversation with itself. "I prefer that to a busy café and milkshakes."

"I bet." Sergio and Kara were renowned for their weekly milkshake dates. Their Domms joined sometimes, too, as well as whoever else they managed to guilt into it. "Mónica is dropping by later today."

She'd texted me while I was in the shower. There were a couple portfolios she wanted me to check out, but we both knew she had an ulterior motive. Since that ulterior motive was about protecting Eli, I didn't fight her on it.

Eli stared at me, forgetting all about plating the food. "What are the rules, Mistress?"

I took a deep breath. I really didn't want to move too fast with Eli. It went against everything I preached, everything I believed in. It wasn't responsible, or a good idea, but I couldn't help but respond. Eli's submission wasn't something it had to concentrate on. If anything, the opposite was true.

"You know Mónica," I pointed out. "Same rules as in the club. You do what she says unless you safeword."

Mónica played with others, but not without Kara either present or nearby. It wasn't that Kara had a problem with it. She'd babbled about it plenty the few times I'd taken her out to have lunch with me. But Mónica was the softest Domme there was, and she needed her sub's snuggles after a scene.

That was to say, I knew there was not going to be any play between them. Eli should, too, but I didn't know if it was thinking clearly enough. The warning was still relevant. Mónica might not order Eli to get on her lap, but she'd have questions.

I'd be the one with questions if she didn't. Making sure subs were all right when they entered a new dynamic was what we did.

My phone buzzed. I ignored it as I rounded the kitchen island to pick up the tray. Everything was on it, as far as I could tell. "Thanks for the food, slut. Now go sit at the table."

Eli frowned. "Sit?"

"We can talk about kneeling some other time."

Eli's knees still needed to heal, and I needed to get proper cushions. I used to have a couple, but I hadn't brought anyone here in so long, I had no idea where I'd stored them.

There was a lot to consider with Eli here. A lot of routines to shift around and settle into.

"Yes, Mistress."

I sighed. I traced the contour of its jawline. "You are doing good, Eli. I just need you to trust my pace."

I was still debating on whether or not this all was a good idea.

Of course, I didn't say that out loud. Some liked to blurt out everything and put it out there. I'd never let anything fester, but I liked to do some inner work before I brought something up. It wasn't Eli's responsibility to take care of my own hang-ups. It applied to Eli, too, but that wasn't the concern now. Eli knew, too. It was yet another reason why everyone was convinced that we were compatible and kept pushing the idea into my head.

Everyone but María.

Whenever the topic came up around her, she just plastered on a smile and nodded along. It was quite noticeable

JUST ONE RULE

when it came from the biggest sunshine of a person there was.

I didn't know how I was going to tell her, either, when I made up my mind on what this was to begin with.

Speaking of, my phone buzzed with a text from her.

> **MARÍA**
> Are you going to play this weekend?

> **ERIKA**
> Yes.
>
> I have to talk to you first, though.

> **MARÍA**
> Everything all right?
>
> Is it about Eli? I saw the thing about its pronouns. Is it just for play or outside of a scene, too? It didn't specify

> **ERIKA**
> It during play. Outside of it, I'll still use it/its, but it's up to the person and the situation. You can ask.

> **MARÍA**
> Okay
>
> Tony signed up to be DM, by the way

I pinched the bridge of my nose. I didn't need to worry about Tony, of all people, this weekend.

> **ERIKA**
> I'll check in with him.

> **MARÍA**
> Okay
>
> Sergio says he's okay with it

> But he's also the one who told me about it, so I'm sus

> ERIKA
> Got it.

Abel's sub needed to get his ass to therapy and actually deal with the history he and Tony shared. For Sergio's sake, and mine. There would be less headaches involved, but Abel insisted that Sergio was coping.

It made me want to punch something at times.

That reminded me of another thing.

But first, I needed to put some carbs back in my body. I was starving after that extra class. Some trainers just demonstrated the moves and spent the class correcting people's forms. I'd always been more engaged, and it bit me in the ass from time to time.

I'd stop if someone needed help with a move, but if I was telling people to do twenty push-ups, I was going to show what doing twenty push-ups looked like.

I slid Eli's chair out for it to sit down. "How do you feel about therapy?"

I grabbed the bowl with Eli's soup and placed it in front of the sub before moving the plate piled up with tempura so we both could reach it. Eli had already placed chopsticks and spoons on the tray.

"Positively." Eli's lips twisted. "I've never been able to afford it."

"Is it something you want, then?"

Eli paused for a few seconds before it nodded. "Is it a requirement to be here?"

"Yes and no." I groaned. I hated that I didn't have a straight answer. "I'd help you get access to therapy even if this wasn't happening, but I'd love it if you found a kink-aware therapist to give you more of a safeguard."

Eli took a sip of the soup as it processed the words. "I'm okay with that, Mistress. Do you have any suggestions?"

"A few. I'll send you a link to a directory."

There were plenty of online options, thankfully, but even for a place as small as this, there were more than a few options for in-person treatment and counseling. León was the one who'd found the directory first, back when he and Danny were struggling to find a balance. I now gave it to anyone I saw struggling or entering a heavier dynamic.

I probably should've brought it up with Eli months ago.

Something else I'd have to explore and beat myself over at a later time.

"Thank you, Mistress." Eli ate more of the soup before it reached for one of the battered vegetables. "I started journaling in one of the notebooks you showed me, too. It's on the nightstand."

I nodded.

Eating together was easy. I was not one for big, loud conversation, and neither was Eli. It worked out. After we were done, I sent Eli to the room with me. I didn't always nap after lunch, but I was selfish and wanted the warmth my new toy exuded.

7
ELI

I want to own every single cell of its body. Eli talked about having everything stripped away, and I understand it's a fantasy, but there's a dark impulse in me that wouldn't be mad if it became a reality.

Mónica came down today. I'm supposed to listen to her. She's the Domme I trust most in our inner circle. I do listen to her. She mostly had good things to say, good-natured ribbing because she still thinks she can get a reaction out of me. The problem is that I don't know what I would've done if she'd had anything negative to add. If she'd said what we were doing wasn't right, would I have walked away?

I don't know.

It's the kind of thing I have to know, though.

- Erika

EMILY ALTER

I took the first real deep breath I'd taken in days the second the doors of Plumas shut behind us. We'd arrived earlier than its technical opening time. I did this with Erika sometimes when I wanted to shoot more content for my site.

It was different today.

After we'd talked about the site and Mistress Erika had teased me with it, I'd mentioned it again. I wanted Her to have more of a hands-on approach when it came to it. She was going to read to me the comments I got and tell me how to pose and what to do for the camera.

My insides were all wobbly imagining it. I was so wet, too. To be fair, I'd been wet ever since Mistress Erika had announced the plan for today. It was hard not to burn the food or to sneak and rub one out, but that didn't feel right. Mistress Erika hadn't mentioned orgasm control exactly—even if I really wanted it to be an official rule—but it had been implied. I'd said I didn't want to do anything She didn't command. Even if She didn't make it a rule, I was not that interested in coming on my own if the possibility of Her making me come was there.

I didn't care what She or anyone else would have to say about it.

But I did worry. Ever since I started to realize that my perfect life would involve 24/7 TPE, and ever since I started fantasizing about Mistress Erika, I'd worried about being able to fulfill all Her needs. But I read Her journal this morning. I hadn't stopped to think about Her worries.

That was bad of me.

"Need help, slut?"

My breath hitched. "No, Mistress."

I just had to finish zipping up. Thankfully, the suit hadn't torn up yet. The other day I was reading a subreddit about people getting holes in their rubber suits around the hidden zippers. I didn't want to have to buy another one. It wasn't even about the money—or not just about that. I bet my subscribers would be happy to finance it if need be, but this was the first gimp suit I'd bought. I took pride in how well cared for it was, looking as shiny and new as the first day I put it on.

After that was done, I made sure my clothes were folded neatly in my locker and shut it closed.

I took a deep breath. Some people didn't understand the appeal in the latex suits, but I found comfort in the tightness, the compression. The invisibility, too. Even if my eyes and mouth were visible, I stopped being Eli the Person when my entire body was covered in black rubber.

I was a shape. Just that.

That wasn't the effect the material had when Mistress Erika wore it. My lips parted when I turned around to find Her there. Her suits were different from mine. For one thing, none of them—because She had different models—covered Her face. She always wore them with high heeled boots, too. The rubber made Her look bigger, more imposing, more authoritative.

Today, She was wearing one of the most covering suits She had, with one large opening that hinted at Her cleavage. It always distracted me way too much whenever She put it on.

"Eyes up here, slut."

Shit.

I gulped. "Yes, Mistress."

There was a glint in Her dark eyes before She cut the distance between us, and then She reached for the zipper that allowed entrance to my holes. "Remember when I helped you do a live cam?"

My eyes widened before I closed them. My heart rate went

up before it slowed down. Everything was right; everything was safe. "Yes, Mistress."

"We're uploading a couple pictures of your front hole, letting everyone salivate on what's to come. Then we're giving them some live content."

I felt more wetness pooling around my opening. My toes curled. It took everything not to sway forward, to reach for Her touch. "Yes, Mistress."

"I think one monthly live cam should be a must," She said. I hummed. I knew She wasn't opening a negotiation right now. We'd talk about it on a more level field tomorrow, or later this evening when we were back home. Talking about it now was part of the fantasy, of the degradation She promised me when we set expectations for today. "It's pathetic enough people are wasting their money on you. The least you could do is show them some appreciation."

My knees threatened to buckle. This. This was what I'd been dreaming about when I asked Her to be more involved with my website.

"Yes, Mistress."

Mistress Erika grinned. She curled Her fingers around the zipper before dragging it down, opening it as far as it went—from my crack to a few inches below my belly button.

The club was kept at a good temperature, but the sudden exposure still made my thighs clench. I gasped when She clutched my groin with that same hand. "Go upstairs to my office. Clear the desk and lie on your back there. Hands holding your knees to your chest."

The command felt like balm washing over my skin. "Yes, Mistress."

She let go of me. I turned around immediately. I didn't zip up again or do anything other than follow Her instructions to the letter.

The desk only had two leather-bound notebooks on top

of its surface. It made sense. Although it was supposed to be a space for admin purposes, I knew Erika took that stuff home with Her. She didn't want to deal with getting Wi-Fi installed here or have anything that held sensitive information and could become a problem. Instead, this was the room where She brought subs to either vet them, have a serious talk with them, or have a scene that wasn't for other people to see.

It wasn't my first time here, but my heart beat as fast as it had then.

I tried to work on it, to focus on my breathing as I lay down like She'd instructed. Seconds passed by while I remained completely exposed in the almost barren room.

My clit throbbed with need. Only air met it, and it wasn't anywhere near enough friction. I squirmed. My fingers tightened around the back of my knees. There was that voice at the back of my head telling me to touch myself, to give in to pleasure. The consequences would be ones I wanted. It would be okay.

I shook off the thought, but my eyes smarted. Crying felt particularly easy this week. I screwed them shut, letting my head loll to the side.

I could obey.

Mistress Erika might enjoy some disobedience for a one-night scene, but She didn't from someone She was serious with.

I didn't want to disobey Her. The thought was repulsive, sending shudders down my spine.

The door creaked open. I knew it wasn't a matter of laziness and not greasing the hinges on Mistress Erika's part. Everything in this room—in this club—was deliberate to toy with a sub's head.

"Mistress." I gasped.

I didn't always care too much about being verbal, but I

did with Her. It was important that She heard the desire in my voice, the reverence, the rightness of it.

Mistress Erika walked farther inside, the click of Her heels against the wooden floor thunderous.

I held my breath for a second. The shutter of a camera clicked. I didn't look to see. Every time She was in charge of taking pictures for me, my views doubled. I was more than happy to let Her do Her thing.

"Hold this to your hole."

I looked when She said that. The object nudged the back of my head.

A violet wand.

I swallowed. I hadn't done any electro-play in a while. I needed more training with it.

Maybe that was why we were using it today—or that was the story I'd go with to keep me turned on.

I grabbed the widest end. I kept my form as I did what Mistress instructed. The toy felt cold against my clit. A shiver ran through me as I imagined the sensation when Mistress turned it on.

Another snap of a camera. I glanced up. It was just Mistress's phone camera. She'd asked me earlier to sign up on my account from Her phone so She didn't have to use mine.

"I'm going to add a quick video. No sound. You just have to turn the wand on when I tell you to."

My lips parted, insides clenching. "Yes, Mistress."

Her making me do it was something else that made everything more intense.

Was this how it was going to go? Mistress switching every scene around to amplify its intensity? My throat dried.

A moan slipped past my lips.

I didn't know how my body would handle the onslaught, but nonetheless I wanted it.

Seconds ticked by. My chest heaved up and down. Sweat began to form around my hairline. I kept my lips parted in an attempt to self-regulate.

"Now."

Her voice was quiet, but it boomed through the room. My heart leaped out of my chest for a second. I found the power button easily. My hands felt clammy, my throat tight.

I swallowed. I didn't want to keep Her waiting, but I fumbled with something as simple as pressing a button. The wand trembled as a result of my hold.

Pathetic, a voice at the back of my head supplied.

It was right.

I was pathetic.

Closing my eyes, bathing myself in that knowledge, helped build the distance I needed to do what I was asked to do.

The zap of electricity was instant. It stung. Burned. My whole body lifted off the desk. I panted. My grip on the wand loosened, the toy clattering on the sturdy wood.

I whimpered. My muscles clenched. My clit throbbed, for different reasons, in a sort of pain it didn't exactly comprehend.

Mistress Erika let out an amused sort of hum. I wasn't sure what it meant, if She was disappointed or entertained by my display. I swallowed, blinking back the sting in my eyes.

"You have a couple of men online already," She said. "Sit up. I'm not recording this part."

I blinked again. I didn't know if my limbs would cooperate, but they eventually did. I moved to my knees, driving my ass back toward my ankles. It was strange, kneeling on a surface where it left me at a similar height as Mistress Erika, but I didn't question it.

Mistress stepped closer. She pressed two fingers against my clit, but Her eyes stayed mostly on the screen. I sucked in a breath, muscles tensing. The pressure grew until I was about to scream. Then She moved Her fingers downward. They entered my hole easily, with no resistance. I curled my hands into fists, my blunt nails digging into the skin. I panted through it as She fucked me with no words—or even looks—exchanged.

It was disconcerting, the seeming indifference as She drove me wild. I could only stare at Her, try and read something in Her gaze.

I couldn't.

The idea that I couldn't only made me clench tighter around Her fingers. It only made the need in my core keep growing.

"DollFucker68 seems to be a big fan," Mistress Erika said casually right as I was straining not to keen over. Mistress knew my body too well, knew the perfect pace and force to drive me wild. It was all I could do to just breathe heavily through it. Her eyes moved to my face seconds later, face stern. "I expect an answer when I speak, slut."

Shit.

Inside, I crawled back, craving a nook to hide under. On the outside, my thighs trembled. I begged for more without words.

"Yes, Mistress." I swallowed, trying to remember what She'd said and guess what She was expecting from me. DollFucker68 was an old man who commented on all my posts, but all the avatars and nicknames blurred together after a while. "He's very supportive."

"That's one way of putting it." She scoffed. I couldn't find it in me to be affected by the dismissive tone. I focused on Her fingers thrusting into me, the waves of pleasure running up my body, spreading. I kept waiting until I wouldn't be able to contain them anymore. "But I guess a slut like you will read how a man wants to use it as a toy until it breaks and find it a compliment."

I hummed. All the words sank deep in my skin. They didn't stick in that negative way that would eat at me, make me question everything. They acted as a cleanser, breaking through every barrier, every wall I built up, until there was nothing to keep me hidden.

"Yes, Mistress."

More.

The words, the fingers fucking into my hole... I'd be happy if time slowed down and we stayed forever.

"Your fans seem to all agree you should show them how you choke on a cock." Mistress shook Her head as She kept reading through the comments. "Men are so basic, aren't they?"

I snorted. Mistress Erika could be funny. I supposed She was right, too. Most of the requests for content wanted to see me choking on a large dildo or fitting that dildo inside my holes. I didn't think twice about it, but they were definitely basic when I compared it to the stuff I saw at the club. Or the stuff that Mistress did to my body, the way She pushed me over the edge, teased every self-imposed limit I hadn't realized I'd had.

"We'll just have fun with that wand another day." Mistress Erika sighed dramatically. Her fingers pulled out of my pussy. A scream got trapped at the back of my throat. My fingers flexed, wanting to reach, to grab her wrist and put it right where it had been. I'd been too close. Every nerve in my body buzzed, trying to grasp that release, that tendril of pleasure still thrumming through my body. Mistress looked pleased, though. That's what stopped me. I was giving Her what She wanted. "I'm going to keep the sound off the live, but I don't want you to talk. Nonverbal cues only."

"Yes, Mistress." I swallowed. I squinted my eyes as I processed what She said. "May I ask why?"

It had made sense on Tuesday. I'd been exhausted from the events of the previous day, and She had sensed it. But under normal circumstances, She didn't discourage me from speaking. I wasn't sure that I wanted Her to.

"I don't want them to read your lips," Mistress explained. "Maybe one day, but today, they don't deserve the privilege of your words."

For a second, I froze. I should fight that statement, rebel against it, but there wasn't even a minuscule part of me that wanted to. Instead, the words washed over me, a balm over every wound that was still healing. It was a different kind of healing, a different kind of comfort.

"Thank you, Mistress."

I hoped She knew what I was talking about. I didn't stop to make sure. It was the kind of question I'd leave for later, after we were out of our latex suits and we reviewed the events of the day. Since we were now in a 24/7 dynamic, I wondered if it should be something we did every day. It didn't feel like too much. In fact, my toes curled imagining the warmth of Mistress's body pressed next to me while we talked. Just talking usually brought forth hives of anxiety, but not with Her.

Not with most of the people at the club, really. Even when I hung out with Sergio yesterday, it had been fine. I understood now what Abel was talking about with Mistress a few months ago. Mistress had been ribbing him about one thing or another, and Abel said that being Sergio's Daddy wasn't exhausting because he didn't expect anyone to match his energy or fill the silences.

"Hop off the desk." Mistress's voice pulled me out of my stray thoughts. There was an amused glint to Her eyes. I wouldn't be surprised if She'd known I was in my head. It didn't happen often, but when I was relaxed enough with someone, part of the appeal of scening with them was the ability to be in my head without any of the negatives that came from doing that the rest of the time. "Let's find you a dildo or two, slut."

My cheeks heated. Only I could feel it, and it was a silly reaction after everything we were doing together.

"Yes, Mistress."

I followed behind Her as She strode toward one of the wardrobes in the main room. It wasn't the first time She helped me record, or the first time She used a dildo on me, so I didn't pay attention to Her selection. Sometimes, I was convinced that Mistress Erika knew my body and my limits better than I did.

I still squirmed once we were back in Her office. It made sense that we returned to this room. For one thing, She'd already set up all the ring lights and the tripod there. For another, Erika wouldn't risk someone passing by while we were recording—even if that person would be a member and fellow kinkster. It would still be a breach. Mistress Erika took those breaches more seriously than anyone I knew.

Without words, Mistress Erika pointed to the desk I'd been on only a couple of minutes earlier. "Kneel first. You're going to coat this dildo with saliva before pushing it inside your wet hole."

I panted, my latex-clad thighs rubbing together. "Yes, Mistress."

I wanted to say I usually had better control, but I wouldn't even know if it was true. I'd started to think that maybe there was a disconnect between the way I actually reacted to things and the way I imagined I reacted to things. I wasn't as put together or well trained as I wanted to think. It wasn't a bad thing, though. Well, I supposed it would be for an Owner who wanted to take me in, but it didn't bother me.

It made me hotter, maybe—the idea that I had to be trained, to be put through the wringer so that I could actually satisfy my Owner.

"I have questions I expect an answer for after this, slut."

I sucked in my next breath. My eyes fluttered closed before I was opening them again. Mistress looked at me with a mix of curiosity and amusement. My gaze darted down Her body. I cleared my throat, shaking my head.

"Yes, Mistress."

"No words starting in five."

I nodded. My throat felt drier than usual, but not completely dry. This wasn't my first live, or my first time using the dildo Mistress Erika had grabbed—a large black one with a wide girth and protruding veins. It felt like a first time of sorts, though. It was the first time Mistress was going to direct me while on a live. The last time She helped me set it up, She just stood behind the camera, recording from different angles. She'd had plenty of things to say afterward about how hot and desperate I looked, but She hadn't said a word while the camera was on.

I was giddy for it and couldn't wait to have Her voice inundate all of my senses.

She placed Her phone on the desk beside me. I was about to ask, but it became clear when She grabbed one of those large condoms from the top drawer and pinched it before rolling it down the hyperrealistic dildo.

Condoms and dams and gloves were a must while in the club, no exceptions.

"You are breathtaking," Mistress said almost reverently, if that was a thing.

I didn't have time to figure it out or to gather a response. I went just as weak in the knees for Her praise as I did Her humiliation, but I often failed to know how to respond to the former. It was probably something I should mention—later, though, when I wasn't holding an extra-large dildo in my hands. The bulbous, shiny head seemed to stare at me as if daring me to embarrass myself in front of it.

I swallowed.

"Can't wait to have that in your mouth, can you?" I didn't need to check to know Mistress was recording already. She'd said the live was muted, but Her voice went an octave lower regardless. I squirmed but looked into the camera anyway. Mistress Erika smirked. "What are you waiting for? There are five men who already jumped into the live the second it connected. Give them what they want, slut."

I glanced back at the dildo. There was no reason to be hesitant.

Hesitant wasn't the right word, either, but it was the best I had right now, when thoughts weren't forming quite right because all my blood was running south. I'd feel self-conscious about it if my neediness was something I struggled with.

It wasn't. Had never been.

I'd turned eighteen, discovered kink, and there had been no room for shame about my libido.

I parted my lips and flicked my tongue out, giving a test lick to the condom-clad dildo. It always felt weird. I was never prepared for the... artificial texture. There was an aftertaste that wasn't there when the thing before me was made of actual flesh and attached to a person.

It wasn't bad, just different. I salivated just the same—maybe more? I didn't know. I wondered what Mistress Erika would have to say about it. I wanted to ask Her but the camera was rolling. She'd said no words. I had to do as She'd said. I *wanted* to do as She'd said. This kind of sex work had never been about me or any misguided ideas of empowerment. It had never been about the men, either, or pleasing them. Maybe it would be different if they were actual Doms, but I doubted even one of them was.

No, this thing had always been about the money and building a safety net in case the worst happened. Now, it could become more. It could be something for me and Mistress Erika.

I liked that idea too much.

Closing my eyes for a second, I got a better hold of the base of the dildo before I wrapped my lips around the head. The sensation was weird. On the one hand, there was hollowness. Sucking the dildo didn't come with grunts, or tensing muscles, or even nods of approval. There weren't any fingers tightening around my scalp, pushing me to take more or keeping me from moving away. There was no feedback, nothing to go on.

On the other hand, all that absence gave sucking a new quality. I didn't even think it could be considered on the same realm. My tongue coated the dildo with saliva. I forced myself to open my eyes again, to look into the camera. Mistress smiled at me. It was the smile She had on when I was making Her proud. I'd memorized it. It had been a rare sight when I'd first propositioned Her to scene together. In the last few months, it had become more and more common.

I wondered if She was aware of it.

There were too many things I was wondering about, I realized. It was interesting. My head should be in the game, in performing for the camera with the dildo Mistress had provided. It was everywhere else, and yet, I didn't hate it. I liked the warmth that enveloped me when I thought of all the conversations we still needed to have.

"I've seen you swallow deeper than that, slut."

Then again... I liked the performance, too. I liked hearing Mistress's encouragement hidden as a degrading remark. I liked the way one side of Her mouth tilted up without Her input. I liked the way Her eyes never strayed from me. I had Her entire focus, and that was heady enough to make me want to prove myself. My entire body buzzed with anticipation, imagining what She'd make me do next, what She'd say next.

I pushed the toy deeper into my mouth. Another difference between sucking on a dildo versus the "real thing" was that I was better at keeping my gag reflex at bay with the latter.

I squinted my eyes; they smarted with unshed tears while a choked sound escaped me.

"You make the most beautiful sounds." Mistress Erika hummed. She'd begun pacing around me, filming me from different angles, I supposed. I just tracked the movement, aware of Her presence, the click of Her heels on the floor. I couldn't *not* be aware. I wouldn't know how. "Pull it out. See how far you can swallow, twice, then place it on the desk and fuck yourself on it."

My body quivered. This was what I'd been dreaming of. Having clear instructions—directions to follow that didn't leave me floundering.

Everything else—all the noise, the doubt—moved to the background when I had an order to follow.

I did as She asked. I didn't choke the second time. I wondered if the camera showed the outline of the toy down my throat, or if I was used to watching too much cartoon porn. I'd never had much interest in watching myself, but... maybe it was something I wanted to explore with the right person.

With Mistress Erika.

First, I had to prove myself, to follow Her directions and show Her what it looked like when the dildo disappeared between my walls.

The stretch burned. The toy was too thick, and even

though I understood the degradation in fucking myself with it, I always preferred the way it felt when someone else was in charge. I got too distracted in the warmth of their body and the knowledge that this was what they wanted to do with my body, the way they wanted to stretch my inner walls.

"Switch to your back and spread your legs."

Yes, Mistress. It physically hurt, not being able to say the words out loud. That feeling was mitigated with the forced stillness of Her voice, the effort to make it sound as if nothing of what I did had an effect on Her.

It made me want to stop everything and worship Her, thank Her, renegotiate everything again so that She had an even bigger role.

In the meantime, I switched positions. My breath hitched —the new angle meant the dildo hit differently, slid deeper.

"Fuck yourself with it fast," Mistress instructed. "Your fans are tipping a lot to see you desperate for cock."

I didn't respond, but I wasn't quiet, either. I couldn't be. It was impossible not to let out a string of whimpers and pants while thrusting the dildo into my front hole, over and over again. I keened and mewled. I wanted Her—needed Her —closer. I writhed, my hips bucking. Maybe I could inch closer to where She stood with the camera. Maybe She'd take over, even if She'd said She didn't want to make Her presence known.

Maybe She'd end the stream after She'd deemed I'd gotten enough tips, and She'd use my body the way I wanted it to be used. I let my imagination run wild with the idea of Her touch. She was right there. I could feel Her. There was a barrier between us, but it wasn't a tangible one. My spine arched as I imagined Her on top of me. When we played in the club, there wasn't always room for a lot of intimacy.

Well. There was intimacy, but it was a shocking sort, a feeling that came all of a sudden when I wasn't expecting it.

It wasn't the slow warmth that built up until it led to an explosion. A part of me said I wanted to experience the latter with Mistress Erika. Another part pointed out that I already had, that it was the reason why everything had felt so right, so natural, so intense with Her these past few months. Somehow, somewhere, we'd stopped playing for the sake of fulfilling our kinks. It had become more.

Did She see it like that, too?

I didn't have time to get more lost in my head, in my fantasy, my retelling of the story I wanted to keep building.

Her hand was there, under my knee. I stilled. I snapped my eyes open. Mistress wasn't holding Her phone anymore. She was just there, watching me intently. She wasn't a primal player, but there was still something animalistic about the way She seemed to devour me with Her eyes.

"What about the live, Mistress?" I croaked.

Truth was, I couldn't care less, but that wasn't what I was supposed to say. I was curious anyway.

"They'll live." Mistress grabbed my hips easily. Wordlessly, I let the dildo slip out of my opening. My hole clenched around the suddenly empty space. It was a weird sensation. Sometimes, I just missed the thing filling me. Other times, it drove me wild with need, desperate to have some kind of relief. "I needed to touch you, and they were all too busy jacking off to keep the tips coming anyway."

I giggle-snorted. It wasn't a sound I was aware I could do, let alone while covered in latex. Mistress Erika quirked an eyebrow. It still took some time to get under control.

"I needed you, too."

It must've been the right thing to say, given the heated look Mistress gave me, infractions forgotten.

8

ERIKA

i've learned a lot since i joined Plumas. i'm not sure if this is the kind of thing you expected to read about from these journals—i might need some clearer directions on this—but it feels important to... put it out there, maybe.

When you first vetted me, i wasn't sure you'd accept my application. You talked so much about agency, responsibility, risk awareness, and community. i went back home, and i questioned everything i thought i knew about kink. It wasn't much, truth be told. when you reached out and said i'd be joining on a trial basis, it was like a weight lifted off my shoulders. But it also brought a lot of anxiety. i didn't want to prove your first impression of me right, but more than that... i wanted to see what all you'd said was about.

For the first time, i wanted someone to prove to me that they knew better than me, and i wanted to learn from them. i wanted to experience kink the way you said it should be experienced and not the way i'd fantasized about it.

Over those first couple of years, there was a lot of talk about you looking for a 24/7 slave. i thought about propositioning you so many times, but i always talked myself out of it. i wasn't ready, i hadn't learned enough to give you what you wanted. no, what you deserved.

i was too fresh.

i guess there are parts of me that are still too fresh. But i've gained so much... confidence, maybe, and it's thanks to you, and thanks to Plumas.

i know you're worried about the timing, and the pace everything's moving at. i understand it, and i respect it, but i'm not the thoughtless sub i was when we first met, Mistress. i owe Plumas that, and i owe it to you, too. That won't change, no matter what.

- eli

I curled my arm around Eli's waist. Aftercare with Eli had never been about being too cooing or extra affectionate, but I still kept it propped up on my lap, held close. Eli had fallen asleep five minutes in. I sighed, reclining back in the armchair. My fingers itched to mark, to double-check that this was really happening.

I kept thinking about the words they'd written earlier today. Eli had handed me the journal after writing in it while I went to open up the gym. It didn't answer all my questions, but I breathed easier as I replayed those written words in my head.

That was what I was doing—working on evening out my breaths—when muffled steps approached. María always came barefoot, or wearing high socks, when she wasn't planning on engaging in anything sexual.

I opened my eyes to watch as she sat on the couch next to mine. I'd moved us to the open area upstairs, where there was a bar, as well as couches and armchairs spread around coffee tables.

"What did you do to Eli?" There was laughter in María's voice as she took in Eli's sleeping form.

There was no sign that it was stirring awake.

Maybe I spent a few seconds longer than necessary watching it, too.

"This week's been too draining." It was the simplest way I could put it. "Some TLC wouldn't hurt."

María nodded. Her hazel eyes glinted for a second. "TLC, Eli edition?"

I nodded. "Mónica and I were talking about setting something up."

We hadn't specified anything. There had been no time. Mónica was a construction manager with workaholic tendencies she wasn't aware of—just because she didn't arrive to work earlier or didn't stay after-hours didn't mean she didn't do ten times more than was strictly necessary. Kara had told me plenty about all the visits and on-site stuff she did.

None of her brothers worked half as much, that was for sure.

The point was, she was busy, and so was I. Between the

gym, managing the club, and now figuring out a routine with Eli, it was fair to say I was beginning to stretch myself thin. I recognized the signs, even though recognizing the signs didn't directly lead to making changes.

"Sign me up."

"Sure thing." I closed my eyes for a second. "Thanks for dropping by."

María chuckled. "Not a hardship. And you said you wanted to talk."

I winced internally. Funny how I'd just been thinking about stretching myself too thin. It was important to talk to María now, though, and not later in front of everyone else. It was the responsible thing and what felt right.

I didn't know if it would change anything, or what it would mean long term, but it wasn't fair to keep her in the dark. Or to catch her off guard.

"Yeah." I scrubbed my face with the hand that wasn't wrapped around Eli. "Eli and I are exploring a more official dynamic."

"Oh." I locked eyes with María. She didn't process what I was saying for a second. Then her eyes widened. She started twirling a strand of her trademark curly hair between her fingers. "That's... good."

It might be, but her words weren't accompanied by that same cheerfulness that had been there when she'd walked in.

I grimaced.

This was another reason why I'd been apprehensive. Things could get messy when people were as intertwined and attached as we were at the club, and I had more power than most here, too.

María cleared her throat before I could think of my next words. "What does that mean for us?"

"That's a tricky question." I hummed. It would be useful

if Eli was awake for this, but we'd talked. I knew where Eli stood. "Nothing has to change when it comes to playing in the club."

María licked her bottom lip. Her open posture shifted, and she crossed her arms. She was wearing one of her lingerie sets—all lace and soft fabric. I itched to ask if she needed a blanket or something to cover up with, but I didn't want to draw attention to it just yet.

It would feel too condescending, and we'd known each other too long for that. María joined the club maybe a month or two after Eli, even though she was a few years older. Still younger than me, but she'd arrived with heaps more experience than Eli, no questions about it.

"I thought you weren't looking for anything outside of the club," María said.

I pursed my lips.

"I wasn't." It was true, but there was more to it. I just had to find the words. "This is still very new. It might not work out in the long run, but Eli presented its case, and it makes sense."

"Oh." I didn't like the sound of that *oh*. "So... that was all someone needed to do? Let you know they wanted more?"

It was a loaded question if I'd ever heard one. Anger rose to the surface before I tamped it down. It was a valid feeling I'd explore later, but it was also uncalled for—more to do with me than the hurt shining through María's eyes.

"Yes and no." I cocked my head to the side as I went over my next words. "Letting me know helps, but it's about more than that."

"Like what?" María pushed the words out.

Her throat bobbed up and down. I wanted to rub my chest —this was already proving more painful than I'd expected— but I remained still.

It killed me to have to be blunt. "You and I wouldn't work outside of the club or in the kind of dynamic I want. You know it as well as I do."

I knew she did, even if I understood that knowledge was now clouded by every other feeling running through her body.

"Yeah." She looked away while her arms remained crossed. "Yeah, no, I get that."

Do you? I didn't pose the question, but it was on the tip of my tongue. It wouldn't be fair to María if I did. This fell on me. Mónica and Abel had been on my case plenty of times about her. I'd known I'd have to talk to her at some point, make sure there weren't any misunderstandings. I'd made plans to, but something always came up. Either someone was going through something and needed my help, or I just lost track of it.

It frustrated me.

I should be able to handle all of it, not make one excuse after another.

"So, what happened? Eli just showed up at your door?"

I snorted. If only she knew how close to reality that bait was. This wasn't the time to tease her, however.

"Close enough."

Eli stirred as I finished giving a summary of the week's events. María didn't take her eyes off me while I spoke. Reading her was usually easy, but I couldn't do it today. She wasn't closed off exactly, but I wasn't sure she was fully here.

"I…" María opened and closed her mouth a couple of times, a frown settling on her face. Eli opened its eyes, rubbing the sleep off them with its fists. "I don't think I can be here."

I forgot all about how endearing Eli looked. Instead, I gasped for air that didn't quite make it to my lungs.

"María…"

It was the closest thing to a plea I'd uttered in I didn't know how long.

"No, I mean, I appreciate you telling me first and all, and it's not on you, and I know technically it changes nothing, but it does, you know?" María let out a dry, ugly chuckle. It wasn't a sound I knew she was capable of making. I would've rather not learned that tidbit of intel. "I mean, there's a difference between you not choosing anyone to have something more with, and you actively not choosing *me*."

I frowned. "I'm... sorry."

María shook her head.

To be fair, *I'm sorry* hadn't been the right thing to say. I didn't feel sorry, exactly. I didn't like knowing that María was hurt by my actions—or my lack of actions. I should've tackled this talk sooner, before Eli got involved or anything else happened. I should've made it clear that while I enjoyed María's humiliation streak, and we worked for casual scenes, there was no long term in our horizon.

She clapped her hands against her thighs. "I'm... I don't know what to think, honestly."

I waited her out. Eli stretched, blinking its eyes open more properly this time.

María froze as she watched. She swallowed. I tried to think ahead, tried to come up with a way to diffuse this. I'd figured it would get messy, but figuring and experiencing it were two different beasts.

"Hi, María." Eli moved off my lap, going down to its knees.

It was what Eli always did when we were at the club. Whether it was me or María, or whoever was there and open for playing, Eli naturally sank down to its knees.

As if working on autopilot, María grabbed one of the pillows on the couch before I could and slid it to Eli. I smiled in appreciation, but I didn't know if it conveyed the message.

I didn't know if it was a message she was receptive to. I couldn't blame her if she wasn't.

"You were really out of it, huh?" María asked in that soft, cooing tone she used with subs after a scene.

She sounded *fine*, but there was pain in her eyes. It was the only thing I could see, the only thing I could focus on.

Fuck.

This was why I didn't overcomplicate matters. I didn't *need* attachments outside of the club. I would've been fine.

Then again... I had to think of this objectively. The fact was, this would've happened one way or another. María might talk about the difference between not choosing anyone and not choosing *her*, but if she'd been hoping for the latter, no matter how much she knew it wasn't going to happen... This would've come up, eventually. The hurt, the strain between us.

I hated it. I hated the way it seemed to fester in my chest, like a weight that was tightening my lungs. I knew it was just a bout of anxiety, that nothing was keeping me from drawing in oxygen, but I still struggled to take my next breath.

Neither of them noticed.

I'd learned long ago to keep my shit under wraps, to survive by not letting anyone see the cracks in the figurative armor.

"Did a live cam."

María forced her face into a relaxed smirk, but everything in her was straining. I saw it, and there was no way Eli wouldn't see it, either. This was not me knowing better or being ten steps ahead. It was clear as day.

"Yeah? That's fun."

I couldn't do anything to stop it, though. I was frozen, just... watching everything unravel.

Eli nodded. No more words came from the rubber-clad sub. Eli just moved to rest its head against my thigh. Eli had always been the kind of sub who needed a time out after a scene; it recharged with quiet, low energy around.

"María."

Saying her name hurt. The gaps between my ribs hurt. Air still felt like a struggle.

Her gaze shifted up to meet me. Her eyes were glassy, gemlike. I breathed out.

I couldn't afford to let go, to let those cracks show. That wasn't my role here. It wasn't what people expected or what they wanted from me—María included.

She wanted a Domme who gave her the physical pain she wanted, but she didn't want the Domme who wanted to own, who wanted to push farther in all areas of her life. I got it. I respected it. I knew my kinks weren't the easiest to navigate. Hence why I'd been happy to just have play partners within the walls of the club I helped found.

Hell, I owed María for helping me accept that part of myself. We had a history that went beyond pain sessions and writing down punishments on her body when she was buzzing with the need for more.

"Yeah?" María chewed on her bottom lip. Her eyes softened around the corners. I didn't think I deserved that... sympathy? I didn't know. I didn't want to read into it. "I'm happy for you, you know."

Yeah. Because she was too kind for her own good. It was something I'd told her plenty of times. No need to stir those memories up.

"If you're uncomfortable with this, we can keep our distance while in the club."

Not forever, but I didn't need to say that. I'd probably consider forever, too. The club was the priority, and María was a big part of it. She'd been with us for years. Everyone loved her. She was an integral part of the family we'd all found here. I didn't want her to become another kinkster who left the community because of a bad breakup or drama they couldn't handle on their own.

I refused to let that happen.

"Don't be ridiculous." María almost laughed. Almost. "I've seen you play with Eli more than anyone else in here. I don't expect you to go all prudish to spare my feelings. I'm a big girl."

Her voice almost broke with that last line.

I grimaced. It was that or huffing in frustration.

I knew I should've gone slower. "I would. If it helped you."

If it kept you here.

María shook her head. Her curls bounced around every time she did it. There was a hypnotic quality to the movement. "I don't want you to. I just... I know you want me to tell you all about reparations and all those big words, but I... I need to process first. Okay?"

My heart pounded against my chest. I kept a cool head, though. I had to. It was the thing keeping me whole.

"Don't disappear." That was the most important thing. I had no right to demand it of her, but I still inflicted sternness in my voice. "This place needs you."

María cocked her head to the side. Her lips twisted up. "You think I'd stop coming here? I spend almost as many hours here as you do."

"Precisely why." I pinned her down with just one look. "We've seen it happen before."

"And we've both sat down and ranted and agreed it was stupid," María retorted. I always forgot how infuriatingly stubborn she could be. "I'm many things, but I'm not a hypocrite."

"I didn't rant," I pointed out. "And it wouldn't make you a hypocrite."

"Please," María scoffed. For the first time, though, there

was genuine humor laced in her voice, in the glassy shine to her eyes. "Look, I don't know about playing any time in the near future, but... I have friends here. People I consider my family. Even if I wanted to become a hermit, Sergio and Kara would drag me here kicking and screaming."

I snorted. That was a funny visual. It was plausible, too. The two Littles were forces of nature on their own, but together? Anything and everything could happen when they weren't supervised.

I didn't stop to process what she said about not playing. A part of me was crying at the loss. Another part was busy reminding myself not to be an absolute asshole. María could at any point in time say she didn't want to play. I didn't own her. I didn't own anyone, inside or outside of the club, even with arranged dynamics in place that said otherwise.

Some people struggled to get the difference, the nuance in it. It was one of my biggest pet peeves. I might go hard on the fantasies, but that was what they were. If I couldn't tell, I wouldn't play with someone.

It wouldn't be right. "And you'll let someone know, if you need some of that dragging?"

María smiled at that. "Yeah. Not today, though. I think I'm just going to chill in the bar area."

"Fair enough." My plan was to be in one of the rooms with Eli, anyway—maybe a few of the others.

It was hard to plan for nights that weren't about a specific kink when there were so many different roles in our group. If it was up to Sergio and Kara, we'd always be in the Littles' room, watching as they colored and Sergio tried to do Kara's hair. Or in the room we used for group play. But the Sadists —and I included myself here—got antsy, and those rooms weren't the ones that had the largest amounts of implements. It meant a lot of moving between rooms as a compromise to keep everyone happy.

Things were definitely easier when there was a planned event. When we'd first started, I'd thought to make all nights a planned event, but both Mónica and María talked me out of it. Something about how people were more flexible than me and I needed to make my peace with it.

Whatever.

9

ELI

I'm shaken up after my talk with Maria. I'm not questioning what I said, exactly. I stand by it. We don't make sense as a full-time dynamic of any kind, but I am questioning other things.

You think we're going too slow, that I'm not giving you enough rules, that I'm not holding the reins as tight as you want. It might've just been a week, but I know you do.

I feel... I feel like I'm failing you, and myself, and... everyone in a way that I know is irrational. But it's important that we have a good base—that I feel like we have a good, solid base.

- Erika

I hated blenders with a passion. Everyone in culinary school looked at me weird when I said it, but they were just too noisy. I had to concede they saved a lot of time, but that was it. Mistress's blender was one of the newer models, so it wasn't *as* loud as it could be. I still wrinkled my nose in distaste while waiting for Her smoothie to get the perfect consistency.

She might've said no to serving Her breakfast in bed—something about how She didn't like lazing around in bed more than strictly necessary—but that didn't mean I was going to slack.

I had Her smoothie, an avocado toast, and the black tea She liked. The first day, I'd added poached eggs, too, but She said She wasn't a fan of super heavy breakfasts, and that meant no eggs.

I only beat myself up over it for a bit because I should've asked about Her food preferences. I'd just assumed I knew everything about Her. Mistress was right when She said there was a lot we had to discover or rediscover about each other. It had started sinking in then.

"Is breakfast ready?" Mistress appeared in the kitchen with a satin scarf around Her hair.

She was already dressed in a pair of leggings and a sweatshirt with the logo of the gym. She'd told me more about Her schedule so I'd know how hungry She'd be each day and plan accordingly. Today she'd be mostly around the floor and the reception area. She only taught one Pilates class, so we could do a lighter lunch.

"Yes, Mistress."

I just needed to pour the smoothie into one of the tall glasses I'd already taken out of the cabinets.

"Good."

A pleasant buzz went down my spine at the praise. It might be me, but I got the feeling that there was more praise since I'd moved here.

It was wild that I'd only been here for a little over a week. I thought I'd be reeling, dissociating to make sense of everything that had led me here. I thought there would be some sense of desperation, of hopelessness.

I wasn't trying to say—or fool myself into believing—that everything was perfect. There was an emptiness, a disconnect, at the back of my head. A vague itch I didn't know what to do about. Mistress had helped with all the logistic stuff, with all the paperwork for everything I needed a copy of, but... it felt strange, like a phantom limb. I might not have been close with my uncle—despite living with him after everyone else threw me to the curb—but he'd still been... a constant. I hadn't trusted him completely, preferring to start an online subscription to have some extra cash set aside, but I had assumed he'd stay.

I didn't regret the subscription, or slipping into the world of sex work, and it wasn't a great loss, objectively speaking, but... it was still one.

I was still figuring out how to feel and what to do about it. Not that I had many choices.

Speaking of... "I have an appointment with a therapist tomorrow."

I cleared my throat. It was too early in the morning for so many words, but I'd just gotten the confirmation email last night, and I didn't see it until I was checking my phone this morning.

Mistress Erika finished a sip of the smoothie before She spoke. She always left Her tea for last. She said She liked it better when it was cooler, so I started steeping it earlier. She was still drinking it last.

"Online or in person?"

"Online." I took a bite of my own toast while building up the sentences in my head. It helped sometimes. Other times, it was more paralyzing. I had learned to tell what situations led to which outcomes. "If it goes well, I'll see them in person."

After wasting my time with two therapists from the list Erika gave me that had had an opening for a brief introduction, I jumped at the possibility of online. I knew me enough to know that in-person therapy would be more... rewarding. But I could only deal with so much disappointment in a single week.

"How do you feel about it?"

I shrugged. I wasn't sure how to answer. I wiped my hands on one of the reusable napkins Mistress had showed me while introducing me to Her kitchen, as She put it.

"Warier than I was on Monday."

It was the most honest way I could put it.

Mistress pursed Her lips in clear displeasure. It wasn't aimed at me, so I let it be. It hadn't been so... bad. I just had assumed that a kink-friendly therapist would automatically be trans friendly, too.

The therapist I'd be meeting later was non-binary. They used they/them pronouns, so I was more hopeful. I didn't know how they'd feel about me switching to it/its with Mistress and the people at Plumas, but their website said that they had experience with people in all kinds of arrangements, from pet players to M/s dynamics with a Total Power Exchange.

It really should work. Now I only had to double-check that they didn't think I was being taken advantage of because of my issues with communicating verbally.

The second therapist I'd gotten a slot with—I might've gone overboard when emailing to set up appointments—had insinuated it. I'd gotten so frustrated, which only made it harder to use my words, and... Ugh.

It was a good thing that I'd thought to ask Mistress if She could pick me up outside.

"I'll be at the café down the street. Just text me when you're done."

I nodded. "Yes, Mistress."

"Good." She leaned over the kitchen island to kiss my forehead.

I blushed. I knew I did. I didn't know how to answer to affectionate gestures like that. They felt good, though.

"Thanks."

"You don't have to thank me," Mistress said before going back to Her toast. "Do you have any plans for today?"

I squirmed. I didn't, really, other than preparing the food for later. "I thought I could text María."

She was my friend, too. At least, I thought of her as a friend. It was strange. I'd kept my life separate for so long, everything in its different compartments, that merging them all now left me questioning the most basic things.

But I highly doubted María didn't consider me her friend. Or someone she cared about, at least. I might not have seen her—or anyone else—much outside of the club, but we'd still talked. María didn't talk a lot about her life either, but she was still more open than I'd been. She'd confide in me if she was feeling under the weather. I'd once baked her a cake for her birthday because she was sad that she couldn't visit her dad.

"I think that's a good idea," Mistress said after a bit.

I'd gotten so deep in my head, I kind of forgot She was there.

I bit my lip. I knew Mistress Erika wasn't texting her. I knew it was hurting Her, too. I just didn't know what to do about it. It made sense to me that María would want—and need—some space apart. Mistress was doing well giving her that, but I didn't know how to take Her mind off it without coming across as insensitive.

I wasn't insensitive to it.

I'd just always been more pragmatic, I supposed. Whereas I'd heard the rumors, the other subs talking about Mistress's relationship with the two of us, I'd always seen her scenes with María as… different. When I'd played with María, it was different, too. It wasn't as involved, as… deep.

Not that I was planning to say any of that.

For all I knew, María wanted some distance from me, too.

THE PLAN I made in my head was to text María later in the day. Mistress was going back to the gym after lunch and a nap She insisted I took with Her. I thought I'd text María then, since I was only planning to make some veggie sandwiches for dinner, and I'd already chopped up all the vegetables and stored them in the fridge yesterday while I waited for the shepherd's pie to cook in the oven.

In the end, I texted María in the morning, shortly after Mistress Erika left the apartment. I just couldn't stop thinking about it, and it was going to keep me distracted all day if I kept pushing it.

But first, I had some texts from some of the others.

> MÓNICA
> How's living with Erika going, sweet thing?

> ELI
> great, Ma'am
> i'm just waiting for Her to trust me more

I was already tapping to exit the chat, but Mónica started typing right away.

> MÓNICA
> I never knew you to be so impatient

JUST ONE RULE

> ELI
> i'm not

I wasn't.

It wasn't fair that Mónica said that.

Ugh.

Well, now I did exit the chat. I'd come back to it later—I wasn't a monster—but I had more people to respond to, and I had to figure out how to open a thread with María. I couldn't say I'd ever been big on texting any of them. I had conversations open with most of the people I played more regularly with, but those threads existed mostly because of the others.

I could admit as much.

> DANNY
>
> Hey Eli
>
> We were hosting Sergio and his Daddy, and he said something about Erika making you socialize more
>
> Anyway, from one fellow sub who gets weird orders to do shit that's good for him or whatever to another, if you ever just wanna chill at the cabin, let me know and we'll pick you up

> ELI
> that sounds good 😊

Neither Danny nor León were demanding people. Those were the best to spend time with, I'd learned. I didn't know enough about Carlos, the new addition to their dynamic—he was at the club most days León and Danny were, but I was usually busy servicing Erika or being teased by María and Mónica. He seemed all right, though. And from what I'd heard, he had his own place here, so he might not even be in the cabin when—or if—I chose to go.

Now, though...

María.

I hesitated as I tapped on her name. The last time we'd texted was about a month ago. She'd texted me because I'd canceled on going to an event. It had been sweet, but I felt bad about worrying her afterward. I'd just been feeling sick that day and hadn't wanted everyone to catch something because of me.

> ELI
>
> hi
>
> are you busy?
>
> it's nothing urgent, i just wanted to check in

I held my breath as I rushed to send the last text. It wasn't perfect. I was definitely not happy with it. Conveying tone through text was hard. Just as with Mónica, though, bubbles popped up right away, showing that María was typing.

MARÍA

Not busy

I'm okay, debating on where to get takeout from

How are you doing?

> ELI
>
> i'm okay too
>
> if you don't want to talk to me, you can tell me
>
> i just worry

MARÍA

You don't have to worry, and you can talk to me

You know I don't bite

ELI

um.

you do bite

I sat down on the couch in the living room before María could type out an answer. I wasn't sure what to think. I guessed I appreciated that she wasn't biting my head off, but there was something weird about the... playfulness. I couldn't tell if it was just a front or if it was genuine.

I supposed I wouldn't struggle with it if I asked to video chat, but that would put a bigger strain on me. It was kind of selfish, but texting was safer, even if it meant some nuances were lost.

MARÍA

And you love it

Did Erika put you up to this?

ELI

no

well, i told Her that i was thinking of texting you and She said She thought it was a good idea

that's it

MARÍA

How is she?

There's been some talk in the group chat, but she's been pretty absent

> ELI
>
> i think She feels guilty
>
> She takes Her role in the community very seriously

> MARÍA
>
> I know she does
>
> But anyway. How did you end up together anyway? Erika was kind of vague

> ELI
>
> i triggered the alarms at Her gym because my phone died and i didn't know where She lived
>
> Abel picked me up and took me to Erika's

I frowned. Had I said too much? Maybe I shouldn't have mentioned Sergio's Daddy. I didn't want María to feel betrayed by him or something. It was bad enough that she and Erika weren't speaking right now.

> MARÍA
>
> Damn
>
> You couldn't wait to see her at the club?

> ELI
>
> i wasn't thinking straight

> MARÍA
>
> Drunk?

> ELI
>
> i don't drink
>
> there was just... family drama

It was probably silly, but María already felt some kind of resentment. I didn't want to tell her that I'd been kicked out and have her use it against Mistress in a bout of anger. It wasn't—I didn't think it was—that I felt like it was something to hide. I knew Mónica had all the details. Abel knew, too, obviously. Even if he hadn't told Sergio, *I* told him when I met up with him. I wasn't hiding it, but...

Maybe it didn't create the best first impression, and it wouldn't create a good impression to someone who might be looking for reasons to turn their hurt into anger.

I was familiar with that kind of thing.

I wasn't implying María would knowingly resort to it, but... Mistress said people were human first and foremost, no matter how much we hated it. I was sticking to that principle.

MARÍA

That sucks

I'm sorry to hear it

But you're doing okay?

ELI

yes

are you sure you're okay?

MARÍA

I'm sure

It's just weird

ELI

because you wanted to be with Mistress Erika?

MARÍA

I mean... I guess

> It just feels like... We're all into polyamory and ENM, and how one person cannot fulfill all your needs and wants, and that stuff right? So it feels like... double the rejection, in a way?

ELI

> i don't want to assume i can meet all of Mistress's needs and wants

I pursed my lips. I wasn't sure if the words rang true or not. Maybe I could discuss it with the therapist tomorrow, if they ended up being nice. In essence, I understood that one person could not fit perfectly with another, that they couldn't be expected to. But wanting?

Yeah, I pretty much wanted to be the person that met all Her needs. I still wanted Her to play with other people, and for Her to pass me around to do the same. But... I didn't know that I wanted Her to do it to get something She didn't get from me.

That was probably unhealthy.

Shit.

I quit the messaging app for a second to write down a note. I definitely had to bring that up with a therapist now. Maybe write about it in the journal, once I had mulled it over some more.

MARÍA

> I'm not blaming you, Eli

> I'm just feeling some type of way about things, is all

ELI

> i don't know what to say to that

I truly didn't. I imagined Mistress would have a better response. For starters, She'd know exactly why She was saying no to more involvement with María. I got why, but I didn't think giving María my observations would help matters.

> MARÍA
>
> I don't expect you to
>
> It's okay, Eli. None of this is on you, and I'm happy you got the Mistress you wanted

It didn't sound like it was okay. I *had* the Mistress I wanted, but I didn't understand what had to be behind María's words. María and Mistress Erika worked together well within the confines of the club and a certain set of kinks. I wanted them to keep working well there, to keep playing and giving each other whatever they needed and wanted. But Mistress was different outside of the club. She had a different energy to Her, different wants. I didn't think María was aware of that difference. I didn't think it was about whether or not María was the perfect fit for Her or not.

The following day, I ended up texting my prospective new therapist more about that than my own history. They were cool with me using the chat in the app for the video call, and it was easier for questions that required long explanations.

"If you had to pick just one thing, Eli, what is it that bothers you the most?"

I held my breath. I hadn't stopped to think about ranking the things that bothered me. I supposed it made sense. I read somewhere that therapists would prioritize the issues to work on.

"Um. I'm scared that Mistress will fall apart."

The therapist narrowed their eyes. They had long hair they'd tied up in a bun and bold makeup around their eyes that didn't take away from the gentleness there.

"And what would that mean for you?"

My lips parted. I knew I'd been gaping for too long when the therapist leaned away from the screen. It was subtle, maybe less than a second, but I caught on to it.

"I think…" I swallowed. Words failed me.

"For now, remember that you can write anything down instead of saying it out loud."

They had a calm voice. It was almost eerie.

I shook my head. I never knew if it was internalized ableism, but sometimes, I felt like saying things out loud was too important, that if I couldn't say them out loud, I just shouldn't say them.

"I wouldn't know how to help. What my role is."

They just nodded. "Eli, if we decide we're a good fit for each other, would you be comfortable with sharing your speech therapist's reports with me?"

"I don't know how."

I hadn't seen her in years. The sessions had been paid by my family, and toward the end of it, there was no progress, no change. I'd agreed to stop seeing her before they'd kicked me out.

"We can talk about that in our next appointment," they promised. I nodded. I hadn't realized, but my heart had started beating faster. "Our time for today is running out, but before we end the call, I want to have a space to give our impressions of each other and how we've felt."

"I've felt good," I answered right away.

My throat was dry.

I was still thinking about speech therapy, my mind trapped there.

They seemed to take note of it, but they didn't call me out. It wasn't as if I was lying. I wasn't. I'd been comfortable. They hadn't cut me off when I mentioned preferring it pronouns because they reflected my kink identity better, or when I described the dynamic I wanted with Mistress. Now that I thought about it, they'd barely asked any questions. It had all come out unprompted.

I didn't do that around many people.

"All right." Ash cleared their throat before smiling softly. "I've felt good, too. I'd love to have a couple of sessions to go through your history before I can make a final assessment and talk about goals and future steps. There's only one thing that strikes me as worrying right now."

Shit.

I looked down.

I'd gone too hard talking about Mistress, hadn't I?

"It's nothing big, Eli, but you mentioned that your Mistress asked you to try therapy as part of your contract with her, is that right?"

"Right," I croaked.

I pursed my lips. I didn't understand the issue there. Lots of dynamics added the caveat of people going or having gone through therapy. I'd even seen kink communities that didn't accept a new member unless they agreed to therapy.

"I just want to make sure that our therapy sessions are not dependent on your relationship with her. So, can you guarantee that you could continue this process, regardless of your relationship?" They leaned forward. They wore a lot of highlighter. It reflected on the screen. "We can talk about payment plans if that's the issue here."

I chewed on my lip. Mistress Erika had said She'd cover the sessions, but I could do that if something happened. It was nice not to stress about how I shouldn't be using the money I was saving up for an emergency, but... Even if Mistress hadn't said anything about the financial aspects of it, Her push would've been more than enough.

"I could pay." I gulped. "And continue therapy."

The idea of it was intimidating, but I could do it.

"Okay. I appreciate that, Eli."

I nodded. They explained how to contact their office if I wanted to set up a proper appointment now that we knew each other, and… that was it.

I didn't know how I was going to do, but I breathed out as I closed the lid of the laptop I was borrowing from Mistress. I felt… accomplished. I needed to sit with the feeling for a bit.

10

ERIKA

Therapy is strange. i think because i was used to speech therapy, i didn't realize just because the word therapy was in it, that they wouldn't be the same. It's good. Just... strange. Ash is nice, even though they have the most stereotypical name ever. They just laughed when i mentioned it.

Ash says that they don't care if i hold all the power or none of it. They care that i know that i can hold the power, and that i have the coping mechanisms to do it if iI ever need or want to. It's strange to think of it on those terms. i mean, I know i could look into getting a job in a kitchen somewhere while looking for a position as a home chef. And i could share a room somewhere just from what i make online, or well, i could if i posted more there. But i don't want to. i don't think it's wrong. i do know the things i want.

- *eli*

"Okay. Spill." Mónica sat down on the couch to my right.

She was wearing tall leather boots I knew Kara had helped with, but she was wearing jeans instead of her usual leather pants. I would've already berated her about it if I wasn't so deep in my head.

León leaned forward from where he was perched on the arm of the same couch—because why would anyone here sit properly on a chair?

"Yeah. Do you know how painful it is to gather intel from Sergio?" He clicked his tongue.

His eyes sparkled, though. León wasn't dressing much more appropriately than Mónica was, but to be fair, he'd never claimed to be into any particular kind of gear. He was just the club's primal player and Sadist. He and I were two of the most Sadistic out of everyone who had a running membership.

The main difference would be that primal play was one of the least appealing things to me—the same way he felt about high protocol. He could be a good listener, though, and his perspective was one I tended to appreciate, what with our similarities and differences.

"There isn't a lot to tell." I sighed.

There was a lot to tell. I just wasn't used to being the center of attention like this. My gaze drifted to the door to the Littles' room where all of our subs would be scheming and gossiping.

"Danny and Carlos are on babysitting duty," León remarked. Of course he caught where my gaze went. "No one is going to come running here while you're pouring your heart out."

JUST ONE RULE

I supposed not. I didn't mind if it happened. It was just… strange to think about.

My stomach churned. "I feel responsible for María."

With that admission came a stab of guilt. I should be focusing on making things work with Eli. I should be making plans to up its tasks, to give more rules, more routines, to carve everything in stone. Instead, I kept going over every time I played with María, every time I led her on, willingly or not. Every time Mónica and Abel mentioned she was clearly crushing hard on me and I'd dismissed it.

León cracked his knuckles. I watched him.

"Why?"

"I ignored the signs, that what we did meant more for her than it did for me."

León blew out a breath. "So you don't feel anything for her?"

"Of course I do. I adore her." I ran a hand through my hair. I needed to get an appointment soon to redo my braids. "I just can't give her what she wants from me."

León hummed. "What does she want from you?"

I huffed. Had I mentioned—recently—how infuriating it was when fellow Domms behaved worse than the brats they were supposed to tame?

"A Sadist to keep her in line."

"And you can't do that?"

"I'm not interested in doing that," I clarified. "I can spank her pussy all she wants while we're here, and I can dole out a punishment, but outside of the club? When I'm home? I don't want someone to keep on a tight leash, to keep reminding of the rules. I want someone who's just there to follow them."

Someone like Eli.

Someone I was taking for granted, not doing even half of the things I was expected to be doing.

"And she knows that, Erika. She just needs a bit to lick her wounds in private," Mónica said.

"Does she?" That wasn't what I got from her texts with Eli. I'd told Eli there was no need to show me the texts, but the sub had insisted, saying it wasn't sure it was doing the right thing. "You talked to her?"

"Kara and I have paid her a few visits," Mónica revealed with a shrug.

It shouldn't have, but it still floored me—which, in turn, added another wave of guilt. Of course Mónica would be checking in on María. She was the Domme I trusted the most for a reason. Despite her brattier tendencies, she was as diligent as I was in making sure everyone was okay and taken care of. Hell, she probably took better care of everyone than I did.

"And she gets that? Because my understanding is that she resents me for not making her part of a triad with Eli."

Mónica grimaced. "She was hurt, lashing out. She might still lash out for a bit, but she understands, just as we do, that there's a difference between someone not having to fit perfectly, and someone not fitting with your core kinks."

León nodded. "Yeah. I mean, I would've kept seeing Carlos regardless, but it would've just been… having a drink at the bar and whipping his back from time to time here or at the cabin. He became a part of us because of how he reacted to our core kinks."

I grunted. León was still in that New Relationship Energy with Carlos even if months had passed since they'd introduced him to the club and I'd made him an official member.

I had to admit they really fit well together. Carlos was much quieter—the first impression I got of him, he reminded me of Abel. A submissive version of my friend, at least. He didn't have that posturing León and Danny were renowned for, but he had an assertiveness to him. All the subs had started to be drawn to it, as soon as they confirmed he wasn't as *scary* as the other two.

I imagined they saw him as a big brother of sorts. I knew Carlos topped Danny and was higher in that... hierarchy, for lack of a better word, but he didn't identify as a Dom or a switch.

Primal players were that annoying.

The point was, I saw how Carlos had gone from a play partner to becoming something more intricate with the two of them. But I didn't see that transposing to what was going on with María.

There were no core kinks in common, no solid base to build from, even if she made a great play partner when I wanted someone's skin to bruise black and blue.

Knowing didn't ease the knot in my stomach.

Just because I was stern, or I showed my emotions less, didn't mean I didn't have those emotions. It didn't mean that I enjoyed seeing others hurt or that it didn't affect me.

I cared about María, dammit. We'd known each other for years. She'd confided in me about... everything, really. I'd let her see more parts of me than I did other people I just saw as members of the club, too.

Mónica rested her hand on my shoulder, squeezing it. "I know you don't want to hear this, but beating yourself up over it is not going to change anything. *You* can't make this better. It's all on María."

I glared at her. It didn't matter that I knew she was right —deep down.

Before I could rebuke anything, the door to the Littles' room opened. Carlos came out, striding straight toward us. Mónica and I exchanged a glance before we watched as he kneeled by León.

It looked... wrong, with León perched up on the arm of

the couch as he was, but it weirdly fit them better than a more traditional stance.

"Sir."

León smirked. I'd bet anything a part of him wanted to tell Carlos there was no need for kneeling, but he was getting better at pushing that instinct down. I approved when he just grabbed Carlos's chin and tilted his face up. "What's up, Sarge?"

Carlos—a retired colonel, not a sergeant—narrowed his eyes. I didn't know the full backstory, but I knew it was a whole thing between the two of them.

He didn't falter. Didn't lose his posture, either. "Kara and Eli seem interested in heavier play, Sir. Danny said it's fine, but I don't feel comfortable monitoring all of them."

Huh.

I exchanged another glance with Mónica. She quirked an eyebrow. Our subs wanted to play heavy? She grinned before we exchanged a single word.

"Dan knew damn well you weren't going to be *fine* with it, and he's just screaming for a punishment." León snorted. He shook his head in fond exasperation. "You did good coming here."

Carlos's body slouched forward for an instant. "Thank you, Sir."

It was León's turn to exchange a glance with us.

Yes, we were all definitely on the same wavelength.

"Let's give those subs what they want then," Mónica said.

For once, I was happy to just follow her lead.

Entering the Littles' room was always an experience. Anything could happen, and it wasn't an exaggeration. If everything was running smoothly, it would just be Littles coloring or playing with the pups, sprawled around the mats. Other times, they could be wrestling—consensually. Or they could be in the middle of some plan that involved us Domms, whether we liked it or not.

Well, we did, but letting them know that was never a good idea.

Littles could be trusted even less than brats. One ounce of power, and everything was lost.

"Ma'am!" Kara hollered the second we walked inside. She'd been on Danny's lap, who was wrapping her up from behind, but she squirmed free to throw herself at Mónica. "You're here!"

I could tell from how Mónica's lips twitched that my friend was trying hard not to laugh while grabbing the Little one. "Where else would I be, baby girl?"

Kara giggled predictably. "Dunno."

Mónica shook her head. "Danny behaved nicely, baby girl?"

The sub nodded right away, effusively. "He's the best, Ma'am. But he kept tickling me, which is unfair. But also fun."

"And... let me guess," Mónica drawled. "Tickling made you horny?"

At this point, and after how long Kara had been with us since she'd moved from the US to our small community in the north of Spain, it was no surprise that's what would've happened.

Unlike Sergio, Kara wasn't a particularly sexual Little, but she was big on group play and sharing of any kind. And certain things were big triggers. Tickling was one of them.

"Maybe?" She rubbed her thighs together, her cheeks red as I hadn't seen them in a while. We should make space for more group play events. When Kara was there, they were the most fun. As if remembering where she was, she turned to me next. "But Eli was horny, too, Ma'am—Mistress."

I shook my head. Kara would never stop struggling with

the honorifics to refer to me. At this point, it was just endearing. It would be weirder if she suddenly started following high protocol perfectly. I didn't demand that as a requirement to step into Plumas, anyway.

"Eli's always horny, little one," I said in my flattest tone while searching for my slut.

Eli was on the floor next to Danny, on its knees. Danny was saying something in its direction, but I didn't catch it. It made Eli press its legs closer together.

León brought attention to it before I did. "You know, boy, having Kara give you a five stars endorsement is kind of pointless if you're gonna be whoring yourself out the next second."

Danny sat straighter. Something else farther south straightened, too. The humiliation slut in him was the quickest to respond to any verbal stimuli I'd seen around.

"Sorry, Master."

León *tsked*. "Right. You're so sorry."

Tag teaming with León to humiliate someone was fun, but I focused on Eli instead. One snap of my fingers, and Eli moved toward me, eyes on the floor until it knelt between my boots. Knees spread apart, gaze down but head held high, chest proud.

Eli was in a full gimp suit, the outfit it always donned when in the club. Only its eyes and mouth were visible.

"What are you horny for this time, slut?"

I kept my tone impassive, even when I couldn't wait to see what would come out of those thin lips of Eli's.

Eli whimpered, eyes darkening with lust.

"Mistress."

"Yes, slut?"

Eli didn't answer right away. I waited it out. Eli knew that was what we did. I didn't care about waiting or using other means to communicate. I cared about people guessing what it was Eli wanted to say. Even if they got it right, or it was obvious, it felt disrespectful.

"I want to prove myself, Mistress."

Hm.

I curled my fingers around Eli's jawline. Eli wanting to prove itself meant being pushed in front of people, to test how much of something it could take for me.

I turned to Kara without giving my slut an answer. "What about you, little one?"

Not surprising anyone, Kara let out a small squeak before leaping closer to Mónica. I admitted it was hard not to laugh.

Mónica wrapped an arm around her while she tilted her head up. Kara had really grown a lot since she walked into our club with Sergio that first day.

"Um. I'm very wet, Mistress."

Mónica took over for me. "Well, that usually helps."

León and Danny snorted. Danny had stood up and was now elbowing Carlos for some reason. I didn't care enough to find out.

Kara pouted, foot stomping on the wooden floor before her brow relaxed. "Maybe Eli and I can be fisted. Or something. Just an idea. Obviously. You Dommes know better and all that." She looked at Mónica as she spoke.

Uh huh.

"So which one of you three came up with that idea?" I asked.

"Why am I being dragged into it?" Danny protested right away.

I pinned him with a look before León could handle him his way. "Because Kara's a terrible actress, and the only times she's asked for a specific anything is because someone dared her to."

Not that Kara wasn't the queen of fisting. She just wasn't as naturally brazen as some of the other Littles and brats.

"Well, I didn't say shit about fisting," he grumbled.

Cute.

León grabbed his face before he could take his next breath. "I'm sorry, was that you volunteering?"

"Huh?"

Our beloved tatted up Sadist just shrugged, eyes narrowed as if he wasn't about to floor Danny. "I was about to say you and Sarge could fight it out, but if you're that insistent…"

"That's not fair." Danny grumbled some more. "Whatever. But they have to do anal, too. In the spirit of fairness."

That little fucker.

León glanced at Mónica and me. I glanced at Mónica. Eli didn't have a preference—if anything, it usually picked anal when given the choice. Most of the times we fisted Kara, though, it was vaginal play.

Kara squirmed. "Can I have a toy for my clit?"

"Don't see why not, since, in *the spirit of fairness*"—I mimicked Danny's words back at him—"he's going to be getting his prostate drilled the entire time and you aren't."

Sure, we all knew the internal side of the clitoris was indirectly stimulated by the pressure against the walls. But indirect stimulation was not the same as very direct pressure against a prostate. Some people preferred it, but that was a whole different thing.

"I wasn't going to say anything," Danny mumbled.

Carlos shook his head. "You really don't know when to shut up."

"I was shutting up."

"Uh huh."

"Anyway." I clapped my hands. "You four, behave for Mónica. León, come help me carry some swings in here."

We could cover the mats, but I didn't feel like being on my knees that long, and the group play room was in use for a private party who'd rented it last month. They were a group of straight people who had joined when the club started and before rumors circulated that we were a safe haven for queers. They still hung out around here, but we didn't interact a lot.

"Yes, Ma'am." The fucker winked.

It took less than five seconds before León asked, "We're turning this into a competition, right?"

I pretended to be exasperated by the question. "How else is my sub going to prove itself, León?"

He just laughed. "Fair enough. That means you're finally going to go harder on Eli?"

I sighed. There were some swings in the rigger room that weren't bolted to the floor—foldable ones that could be moved relatively easy. They were just bulky as fuck.

"Going hard on Eli when it comes to a scene has never been the issue."

That wasn't changing, either, as far as I was concerned.

11

ELI

Carlos rushed in to help as Mistress Erika and León walked through the door. They were each holding a foldable swing in one arm, and a third one was shared between the two of them.

Carlos grabbed that one.

"Thank you, boy," Mistress said.

Setting them up was quick. They'd all been used before, but Mistress and León both double-checked every screw and made sure they were sturdy. I'd been antsy while She was gone, shuffling closer to Mónica without realizing. Before this week, I usually leaned toward María if I found myself alone in the middle of a scene. Mónica was a good Domme, too. She didn't say anything of my approach.

Mistress locked eyes with me. I knew She noticed the shift, but She didn't mention it, either.

It made me squirm more noticeably. I wasn't scared about scening with Her. There was none of that anxiety that had accompanied me the first few times we'd played together. Back then, before things actually started, I'd have to fight off nervous energy—voices in my head saying I was going to prove Mistress's concerns about me right if I wasn't careful.

Now, the beginning of a scene wasn't anxiety inducing. It was like walking somewhere warm, somewhere safe and inviting. The middle of a scene was my safe space.

I still lingered, not fully relaxing until all the swings were in place and Mistress signaled me to approach.

"All right. Listen up, subs." Mistress clasped Her hands behind Her back. "We're keeping it simple here. The three of you will be tied up to the swings. First to come gets bragging privileges and a drink of their choice."

"Do milkshakes count?" Kara piped up right away.

I closed my eyes. It was so easy to laugh when one of the age players spoke, but I had to focus.

"Yes, little one, unfortunately." The dry tone was somewhat forced, but it made Kara giggle anyway before jumping onto her swing.

Danny climbed up next, with more grumbling for good measure.

"You're so fucking lucky Kara is here, Dan." León chuckled before he leaned toward Carlos to whisper something in his ear.

Only Mistress's actions were important, but I couldn't help but observe everyone else.

"I don't know," Mistress mused. "I'm sure the five of us can stay longer and spice things up."

León winked at Mistress. She wasn't often this playful, but I liked when She was. I also liked the hidden promises in those words. Impact play or heavy pain were out of the question in front of Kara. We didn't engage in someone's hard limits when they were anywhere near. But a competition with Danny?

I'd seen him do those with other masochists, but I'd never taken part. It had always been established couples, so even though I'd considered asking Mistress how She felt about it, I always chickened out.

Not now.

"Get on the swing, slut."

Right.

Fisting competition.

I swallowed. I wasn't scared of fisting—I liked the stretch, the pressure, the pushing through what seemed like my body's limits at first glance—but I didn't know how I was going to win. I could come fast, but that was usually from clit stimulation and vibration, not from penetration. I could come from it, but it took longer.

Anal did make it easier, though.

I closed my eyes before standing on my feet. Mistress helped stabilize me. She guided me to the swing, too, then turned me around and lifted me into the leather seat. I pulled my legs up, bent toward my chest so she could attach the dangling cuffs to my ankles easily. Mistress didn't say, but Her eyes glinted with approval.

Sometimes I thought I preferred that kind of silent praise, the one I knew wasn't forced or fabricated for the sake of it. Mistress was proud of me.

"Mistress." I breathed out the word as she finished clasping my wrists to the top end of the triangular device.

"Quiet," She ordered, but Her hand wrapped around mine right after She spoke. "Can you do that?"

Without questioning it, I gave one squeeze. Mistress pulled back.

She unzipped the opening in my suit to my ass and spread my thighs farther apart. There were steps around me, around us, but this time, I didn't look around. The second I hit the leather seat, my brain decided it was the start of the scene, and that meant all focus went to Mistress Erika.

León appeared in my vision field. He handed Mistress a

bottle of lube and a pair of nitrile gloves. My heart thrummed a bit faster as Mistress placed the bottle next to me and pulled at the glove. The latex stretched around Her skin before clinging to Her Hands, Her arms. I loved these kinds of preparations. They almost felt ritualistic, with a hypnotic element to them. I squirmed in place, not that I had a lot of room to do what I wanted—to get some friction.

It was enough that the chains that connected to the rods clattered, though.

Mistress had Her eyes on me right away.

"I don't appreciate impatience, slut. You know that."

I shivered.

Yes, yes I knew that. Hearing it was what I needed to quiet all the thoughts rummaging in my brain.

"That's right," Mistress said. It must've been transparent on my face, in my body, the second Her words sank in. It was a good thing. I didn't want to hide anything from Her. Seemed counterproductive. "Now, I know you don't care about milkshakes or bragging, but you do care about making me proud, don't you?"

Air left my lungs. I bobbed my head right away. The latex squeaked against the leather, but it didn't matter. It was never a sound that had bothered me. If anything, it made me feel more of an object and less of a body forced to be present in a specific point in time.

"Good."

There were other murmurs, if I focused enough. Whispers, and soft snorts, and mewls coming from both sides. People tended to disappear around me even when I was playing in a group, but this felt more. They weren't even in the background—they were somewhere more distant, more irrelevant.

Only Mistress was within reach.

My chest rose and fell rhythmically as I watched Her. She

was diligent in how She squirted copious amounts of lube on Her gloved fingers. She massaged the substance, warming it up, before even getting close.

"You look perfect," She said.

I glanced down as She circled the wrinkled skin around my hole. My breath caught. I had to breathe, had to stay calm. Mistress wasn't slow. She didn't take Her time, but She would not be rushed. It was one of the first things I learned about Her. It didn't matter how much someone ribbed Her about how slow or fast She was going. Her pace would not break. She would not be deterred.

A deeper grunt—Danny's—jolted me. I didn't want to look, to be distracted by something else, but...

"Look at him, slut." As if reading my mind, Mistress was right there. She used the hand that wasn't teasing the entrance to my ass to turn my head to the side. A finger breached me as I obeyed, as I tried to get my eyes to focus on the figure on the swing. I panted. "I told you to be quiet. I didn't tell you to go shy on me."

I pressed my lips together. My eyes widened. León had two fingers inside of Danny, but that wasn't what had him grunting, eyes screwed shut, mouth twisted in pain. León had his other hand on Danny's pierced cock, applying force, squeezing.

"You think you can compare to him?" There was derision in Mistress's voice, but there was more to it.

Curiosity, maybe.

I didn't answer. If Mistress wanted me to, She'd tell me. She'd lift the command to be quiet.

So I didn't.

I focused on Her finger instead. Mistress's hands weren't too big, but they were strong, and Her fingers were long. She wasn't rushing to add a second finger, but She thrust in and out, pressing against my inner walls. The movements were simple, measured, slow. I didn't understand why it was overwhelming and threatening to send me over the edge. It was nothing I hadn't done before, but it felt bigger. Overwhelming, almost, in its simplicity.

To my right, buzzing started. I could hear high-pitched moans and whimpers. I panted. Mistress smirked at me as if She could read my mind.

I wouldn't be surprised if She could.

A second finger was added. My body clenched at the new intrusion and tried to curl in on itself. Mistress waited for me. I didn't make her wait long. Relaxing my body for her was almost instinctual. It was the easiest thing to do, the most natural. My chest heaved with the extra effort, but it didn't matter.

I could feel that wave of endorphins getting closer, ready to drown me. I welcomed it. Underneath the metaphorical water, I didn't have to worry about whether or not my body could take what Mistress had in store for it. There was no room for it. There was no room for questioning the heat building up, my heart rate, the way everything in me ached and begged for more. There was just feeling and Mistress.

It was a different way of being present within the corporality of my existence. I was connected to every fiber of my being, every sensation that zapped through my skin. Only those existed. At the same time, all of those sensations were covered in syrup, in an addictive substance that didn't let go, that made me beg for more without caring that I didn't know what that more meant.

I just wanted to live with that feeling—the knowledge that there was something superior to me making the choices, knowing what my body needed before I could reason through it.

"Can't keep still, can you?" Mistress's voice broke through the haze.

Huh?

I hadn't realized Mistress was adding a third finger. My hips bucked up. I was squirming, moving more than I was supposed to—more than I usually did. It wasn't the first time this had happened.

I didn't understand why, exactly, but staying still seemed harder now that I slept in Her bed. Mistress didn't complain. She hadn't said anything or shown Her displeasure. She just commented on it every now and then when She wanted me to feel those tendrils of humiliation. I screwed my eyes shut. My lips parted. I just needed a second before I faced Her again.

I had theories, but I didn't dare voice them out loud yet. Those theories said that my body craved Hers, that it finally felt comfortable where it lay, confident in being wanted back. A part of me mourned the well-behaved slut who took everything without twitching a muscle. A bigger part admitted there was a freedom in this… newer side of me I could easily get lost in. It was that freedom that had me taking a deep breath, that had air fill my lungs.

I was completely gone by the time Mistress's fingers hunched in that cone-like shape. I couldn't keep track of the others, could barely remember what the rules were for the game we were playing. I flew as the pressure increased and my muscles protested the stretch.

My thighs tensed, quivered. I hated the clank of the chains giving away my tremors—the struggle I wanted more of.

Mistress came closer right away. She pressed against the underside of my thigh, bending me, opening me even more. No sound came, but my lips parted anyway.

Maybe a sound slipped out after all. I didn't know. I didn't care to find out.

The shift in position wasn't huge, but the new angle fired up every single nerve in my body.

Mistress's knuckles brushed against my rim. I could feel the fullness that was almost there, within reach. I pushed against Her hand before She could ask me.

Her hand slipped deeper, pushed harder.

I gasped.

I knew Her fist was inside of me without having to look. There was always a strange popping when it happened, a specific kind of burn when the thickest part of Her hand made it inside and my skin fought for purchase and attempted to adjust to the new shape inside.

"You wanted to prove yourself, slut." Mistress was bent forward. Her lips ghosted over the side of my covered head. The latex around my ears diluted the sound, but it was there. It made my toes curl just the same. I was here, but I wasn't. A tear slid from the corner of my eye. Relief. Gratitude. "I'm waiting."

A shiver ran down my spine at those words. Mistress knew what she was doing with them; She had to. She knew all dams would break; all restraints I'd tried to carefully place would scatter away until there were no shields left.

The only thing left in place was the building pressure, the burning stretch. Franticness clawed at my sides. I became an animal, a receptacle for every feeling, every sensation shoved into me. A channel.

I couldn't tell when I came, exactly. I couldn't tell if I did it before or after someone else.

It didn't matter.

12

ERIKA

Something had shifted. I didn't have any choice but to accept it and respond accordingly.

After the day in Plumas and brunch the next day, it was clear that new rules needed to be added. Eli kept proving itself, and I had to step up. There was no other way around it. Eli was fulfilling everything on its end, and I was the one lagging behind.

It would not do.

Talking with León more the other night helped—after Mónica and Kara had called it a night, and Danny and Eli had both exhausted themselves. Carlos had been cradling Danny in his arms, and Eli had been with them, listening to whatever words Danny was managing to slur together.

León and Danny didn't have a M/s dynamic per se, but Danny ended up behaving like a service sub more often than not, and they played with the roles often enough to make it count.

Or maybe I'd just needed that bout of energy that came from a scene with other Domms, or from spending time at the club without the weight of overseeing a workshop or wearing an arm band that identified me as a DM for the evening.

Whatever it was, it had solidified that it was about time to start pulling my own weight in a dynamic that was all about me wanting to have that weight and that level of control.

"Eli?"

It took less than two seconds for Eli to come running downstairs.

The one aspect of my life where I didn't follow high protocol were clothes. I'd fantasized about it once when I'd first started reading on kink history and learned about the kind of power imbalance I'd crave. Ultimately, though, because of the gym, I wore sportswear ninety-nine percent of the time I spent outside of the club. I loved the power that came from donning the shiny latex, but realistically speaking, I had no interest in changing clothes the second I walked through the doors of my house just to recreate an aesthetic. It made no sense to make Eli wear any particular set of clothes when I wasn't going to do the same, which was why my slave wasn't breaking protocol when it showed up wearing an oversized hoodie and boxers.

I still had to get it more clothes, but for now Eli seemed more than comfortable with the underwear I had express delivered and borrowing old clothes of mine. I couldn't say I hated the look, either.

"Yes, Mistress?"

"Kneel," I commanded after standing up from the couch. "Hands behind your back."

Eli didn't hesitate to go down, its knees thudding against the wooden floor. There was no sign of pain or discomfort at the impact. If anything, the few wrinkles across its forehead faded away. Its eyelids hooded in pleasure at the simple command.

I circled the spot where it kneeled, assessing Eli's—perfect—posture before I spoke. I didn't need to wear any gear or be in any particular location to slip into my own headspace, the one that added a more authoritarian tone to my voice and had me standing taller without any conscious effort on my part.

Entering Domspace wasn't about having all my focus zeroed in on Eli or the implements I was using on its body. I knew it wasn't the same for other Domms, but for me, it meant taking a weight off. In the same way subs got rid of all the stress and anxiety of their daily lives, I got rid of all the weight that came from being too aware of my body and how I presented myself. When I was fully immersed in the roleplay, I wasn't actively thinking about such things. It just came naturally.

"I'm giving you more rules." For a second, before Eli could catch itself, its body sagged completely, hooded eyes fluttering. I smiled to myself. The way Eli seemed to be coming unraveled in ways I had never seen while watching it in the club now that we were shaping a 24/7 arrangement was telling. It was also entertaining, for now. "That is, if you pass a test."

A frown etched its features. "Test?"

Eli swallowed, nerves clearly resurfacing. Its posture didn't falter, though. There were no tremors or any other reaction.

I approved. "For now, assume that any time there's an increase in rules or tasks, there will be a test first."

"Yes, Mistress."

"Good." I stood in front of Eli. It took some effort not to squat down and caress its face. It wasn't a... feeling I was used to. I shook it off. "Take off the hoodie and resume your position."

"Yes, Mistress."

The answer came right away. I'd always noted how the use of honorifics wasn't something Eli ever struggled with. Back when I'd first met Eli, and Eli had explained its issues with verbal communication and speech, I'd poured quite a few hours into researching about it. I'd asked Eli, too, but educating myself had felt important. If only the internet wasn't full of misinformation around everything that had to do with language and people's ability to produce it one way or another. Between the misinformation and the constant infighting, I'd resigned to learning from observing Eli any chance I got.

A part of me was still bothered that I wasn't the expert I wanted to be on it. Eli wouldn't agree, of course. It wasn't so much idolization as the fact that I *was* good at listening and anticipating its needs. That didn't mean I wasn't going to be hard on myself, for better or worse.

"Wait here."

I took a minute to make a quirk incursion upstairs and grab what I needed. In an ideal world, where Domms were robots instead of humans, I would've already had everything laid out in the living room, ready for use. In real life, I kept most of my toys upstairs, in the room where Eli had been. And most importantly, in real life, I didn't plan out a scene hours in advance, allowing for no flexibility.

Well, I did plan scenes hours in advance, but they weren't set in stone. Nothing happened until I was facing a sub and reading their moods, their cues. That meant lots of last-minute changes, lots of improvising and creative thinking.

I shook my head as I grabbed the flogger I'd had in mind for today. It was about time that Eli took over moderating the app. Spending too much time online turned me into the kind of preacher I ran away from.

Anyway.

Eli was exactly where I'd left it, acting like the perfect

object that didn't need to switch positions or got distracted by its surroundings.

"Knees okay?"

There was only a second of consideration. "Yes, Mistress."

"Good," I praised before moving in front of Eli. Its eyes were closed, but they opened when I stopped, looming over its form. I squatted down to place the notebook and pen I'd grabbed to Eli's right. "Ready to hear about your test?"

A hitched breath, then a nod. "Yes, Mistress."

I nodded, too, before standing up. "It's simple, really. While I flog your thighs, you're going to come up with a list of ten material things you want. When you've thought of them, the flogging ends. You can then tell me or write them down."

Silence built around us. One second, two, three. Counting as I waited Eli out came naturally. I'd expected a certain degree of resistance, but that resistance was not enough to deter me. Eli had lost everything only two weeks ago. I didn't care that it had never come across as particularly materialistic. Eli was human, which meant, at the very least, it had wants and comfort items.

"Yes, Mistress."

"Spread your legs wider."

The flogger I'd grabbed was made of a soft leather. It was intended for sensation more than impact play, even though it had a bite when wielded properly. I didn't want to overwhelm Eli with pain—just give it enough to quiet every protest, every fight its brain might try to put up. I was building Eli back up whether my slave liked it or not, and it started now.

I only waited until Eli settled in its new stance before letting the flogger fly through the air. I didn't add a lot of momentum to it. Right now, I only wanted to warm up the skin, to help Eli slip into that headspace where its only purpose was to obey me, to please me.

"You deserve things, pet."

As I'd predicted, Eli's breath hitched, and it had nothing to do with the strands of leather raining down on its thigh.

Praise play wasn't my biggest strength. Even now, I knew I laced the praise with more humiliating aspects than most of the Domms around me. I'd thought about it often. I didn't have a problem with praising someone. It didn't make my skin itch or bring me any kind of discomfort. I just had less practice with it, as... nonsensical as the notion seemed. For years, most of my time had been spent humiliating men for money. It was where I was the most comfortable and where I was the most confident in my skills to achieve the result I wanted.

Praise was different. Bringing someone to their knees was easy. Rewarding, but easy. Praising someone meant putting them first in a place where the words would actually sink in. It required more finesse.

A soft, barely there whimper slipped past Eli's lips. It pulled my focus back. A small shiver ran down its spine. Its bottom lip was trapped between its teeth.

"You deserve comfort." I alternated between Eli's thighs with the flogger, setting a slow rhythm. It was about lulling it into a sense of security, into that safety blanket Eli found in the depth of a scene. "You deserve fulfillment."

Time ceased to exist. Everything narrowed down to the flogger, Eli, and the affirmations coming out of my mouth. All my focus was on its body, its reaction to each strand of leather hitting its thighs. I noted every clench, every flinch, every gasp that came out of its mouth. One thing about Eli was that it had the most obvious tells. The media displayed subspace as something unreachable—as something dangerous to reach, even. It showed subs that reached subspace from one second to another, and their bodies stopped responding. They became muppets with their strings cut off, a vessel that didn't respond to stimuli, that didn't *feel* it.

It wasn't the reality found in the clubs when actually playing with someone, but if a sub ever came close to reflecting that experience, it was Eli. There was a visible, stark difference when the slut reached that headspace that let it breathe more easily. The fight left its body completely as the flogger kept adorning its reddening thighs. Welts rose, angrier lines that had to sting, but Eli just sank deeper. A few whimpers left its lips. Shivers ran down its body. A few hitched breaths. Those were all the signs that it was present and feeling the lashes of the leather.

Watching the skin blossom as it reacted to the leather had a hypnotic quality that should've gotten old by now but hadn't. If anything, there was new appreciation to the ritual of it, the patterns and crisscrosses each strand created against previously unblemished tissue.

I couldn't tell how much time passed. I just kept the rhythm going, drinking in every moan, every gasp, every shiver. I watched as I aimed to cover every inch of skin, as I teased the raised skin where it would burn more with the supple leather. I watched the muscles in Eli's arms clench, the cord in its neck bulging.

This was where Eli belonged—on its knees, receiving whatever I chose to give it.

The thought was the revelation I hadn't realized I needed to reach. It bolstered me with renewed purpose.

I added more strength when I wielded the flogger next, aiming higher so the strands of leather caressed Eli's groin. It didn't matter that fabric covered it. The new angle wasn't about that—not today.

"I'm done, Mistress."

I paused right away, the leather falling gently against Eli's thigh, as if it wanted to caress, to apologize for the abuse it had inflicted.

"Good."

I moved to place the flogger on the coffee table. As soon as I was back, the endorphins that had kept Eli in that headspace that toyed with the physical limits of the body came crashing down. The shivers that had already been covering its body grew more violent. Whimpers grew louder, breaths turned sharper. I grabbed hold of its arms and wrapped them around my neck, then I moved us to the couch.

"Breathe through it, pet." I ran a hand down its arms as I spoke.

Eli scrambled to catch air while keeping a distance between our lower bodies.

"Burns so much," Eli gasped. "It was so… so good. I'm so turned on, my clit's throbbing so bad, Mistress. I—I—"

The more it spoke, the more jumbled the words got as they were mixed in with gasps and silent sobs.

"I've got you."

I did. Wrapping one arm around Eli's middle, it was easy to shift its weight around until its head rested burrowed against the crook of my neck. My lips met its temple as I cupped its groin with my other hand. Whenever Eli was feeling overwhelmed, pressure against its throbbing clit was the thing that brought it down.

"Th-thank you, Mistress." Eli hiccuped. Its hand wiped at its cheeks almost furiously. I wasn't going to rush the slut either way. "I haven't given you the list of things yet."

My gaze darted to the pen and notebook forgotten on the floor. I ignored the itch to pick them up right away, squeezing Eli's waist instead. "Do you need to write it down?"

"No, Mistress." I sat straighter. The answer had been too abrupt not to put me on alert. "I can do it."

It wasn't a matter of whether or not Eli *could* do it. I made a mental note to ask if Eli *wanted* to write it down next time. For now, I nodded. "All right."

I watched as Eli's chest rose and fell, more frantically at first, and slower as seconds passed. It was back to a regular rhythm when Eli opened its mouth.

"I want one of those hoodies that have animal ears on top, and proper kitchen knives, and a knife sharpener." Eli hiccuped. I moved my hand to cup its jaw when Eli moved so it could sit more properly. "And I want platform boots with spikes and a piercing. Maybe two."

"Okay." It was hard not to laugh. For one fleeting second, I could relate to the Daddy types around me. There was something special about having someone making demands while their face was scrunched up red and they weren't quite out of a vulnerable headspace. "What else, Eli?"

I wasn't keeping count, but there was no doubt in my mind that Eli was. Truth be told, I didn't care if Eli went over ten. I just cared that Eli knew to ask for things for itself and there was no doubt in that subby brain that it could.

"You aren't going to get everything right now." Eli gulped. "Are you?"

I sighed inwardly. It wasn't Eli's fault, or mine, but I needed to add more praise and worship. No sub of mine was going to struggle with self-esteem. "Is that for you to worry about, slut?"

The sternness in my voice helped halt the anxiety swirling back up in Eli's face.

"No, Mistress."

I ran a hand over Eli's scalp, resting on the back of its neck. I gave Eli a second to settle before I repeated the question. "What else do you want?"

Eli squirmed some more. I hated that doubts had trickled in. My slut had been doing so well up until now, listing more than I'd expected.

"Um. Noise-canceling headphones." Eli used its fingers to list the rest of the items. I noticed how the words came with more pauses. It hurt to see. "A proper bell so you can call me with it. Weighted blankets. One of those magnetic batteries for my phone. And, um, a vacuum bed? We can have it in the club. And others can use it."

"Done." Interrupting wasn't my first choice when dealing with a sub, especially one like Eli who already struggled to verbalize. It had been... instinctual—a voice at the back of my head telling me it was either interrupting or listening as Eli offered up everything else to be shared too. "You did good, Eli. Thank you."

In response, Eli shivered. I pulled its body close to mine again, letting it burrow against my neck. I always thought that, if I turned any of my dynamics into a 24/7 arrangement with the kind of TPE I wanted, it would be less... affectionate. I was never one for big displays of it, but I couldn't *not* hold Eli; I couldn't *not* offer my slave comfort.

There was some more squirming, some more shuffling around. I didn't hesitate often, but the feeling was right there, crawling underneath my skin. Was I supposed to hold Eli tighter? To give more breathing room?

"You said more rules." Eli's voice came out in a whisper. It might not have been strong, but it was all I needed to pull back. I was beginning to suspect Eli would always pull me back, whether or not that was a good thing. "Now?"

"Yes." I shook my head. Was I being too lenient? Impatience had never been a trait I found particularly endearing. Definitely not in large doses. "But I'm going to need links to either the specific products you want or brands."

"I'll send them to you, Mistress."

"Thank you, pet." I took a second to focus on my breathing. Today was supposed to be about regaining control, but it kept slipping away. It didn't seem to matter what I did. "Come with me to the bathroom."

"Huh?"

"Questioning me, pet?"

It was a tease, but I wouldn't say there wasn't a challenge there. Attitude I needed to hold on to until it felt real again.

Eli swallowed. I'd worry if that was its only reaction, but a placid smile settled on its lips two seconds later. Brown eyes twinkled as it met my gaze. "Never, Mistress."

13

ELI

I didn't know what I was feeling, what was going through my mind—if anything was. I only knew Mistress Erika was there, holding Her hand out for me. I only knew Her voice, the cadence in Her speech as She led the way to the bathroom. My knees buckled, and my thighs quivered. The skin was red, marked with raised welts where the leather had hit. No skin had broken, and it hadn't come anywhere near the pain I could tolerate in a scene.

Maybe it was simply because feelings were involved now, but I felt weaker than I usually would. My head still buzzed with the fight to focus, to think of those things I wanted, to not get lost questioning if what I asked for was fair or if it was too much.

I didn't know that it wasn't, but Mistress had praised me for it. She hadn't been put off, and I trusted Her. I let Her words wash over me—the reminders that I deserved nice things, that I was good. It might not be great that I needed the reminder in the first place, but Ash said I had to give myself grace while we processed everything. They said Mistress Erika was right to be wary with me, that I was in a vulnerable state, even if that didn't invalidate the fact that I knew what I wanted and that I had a right to ask for it.

That was what I understood, anyway. I'd only had one more session, and it had mostly been about my history and background and stuff.

"Eli?"

Shit.

I got distracted.

We were in the bathroom, where She'd said She wanted us to go.

Mistress didn't scold me. She just sat me down on the bidet. The vitreous china was cold against my legs, but it was a cold I welcomed. It acted as a salve against the flesh that was still reddened and pulsing in the aftermath.

I focused on my breaths. Deep breaths, the kinds that lowered my heartbeat and squashed the shivers that still ran down my spine.

I didn't realize I'd closed my eyes until I noticed the shifts in the air of someone walking around me.

Not someone.

Mistress.

I watched as She kneeled in front of me with the first aid kit She kept in the cabinet above the mirror. Mistress Erika was always diligent about aftercare. It meant I didn't have to pay a lot of attention. There were Domms I'd been with who I'd had to explain if something would make a welt sting more or slow its natural healing process. Just because something was in a first aid kit didn't mean it had to be used.

I never had to correct Mistress. I kept my eyes on Her anyway, but it was simply because I liked the ritual. I liked seeing the confidence in Her movements, the no-funny-business attitude as She grabbed the bottle of aloe vera. It was the good, one-hundred-percent natural kind.

There was a reason why She was in charge of restocking the aftercare kits in the club.

Now that I thought about it, She was in charge of most things that had to do with the club.

"Are you with me?"

"Yes, Mistress." My fingers curled around the edge of the bidet. The aloe vera barely left a sting after it was applied, but I still needed the extra support. "Thank you."

"What are you thanking me for?" Mistress shook Her head. There was laughter in Her voice. Maybe something else, or maybe I was overthinking it. "Never mind. I said I was giving you new rules."

I nodded. *Yes, Mistress* was on the tip of my tongue, but I got the feeling it would be distracting instead of helpful. I did want to hear those rules more than I wanted to show respect, anyway. It wasn't something I felt bad about. I'd wonder if that was a good or a bad thing at another time. Right now, I wasn't fully out of that headspace where everything that existed was Mistress. Her fingers on me as She lifted me up both burned and healed the skin they touched.

I blinked. I didn't know why we were moving again, but I didn't fight it. I just followed Her back to the living room. I didn't miss how Mistress paused and took a small detour to grab the unused notebook and pen from the floor.

Should I have thought of it?

I was never too aware of my surroundings when in the middle of a scene. Well, I supposed I *was* aware, but that awareness was selective. I was aware of the people around me—sometimes, when they were there for me. I was aware of the toys they used on me, too.

That was about it.

"Do you prefer sitting or kneeling?"

"Kneeling, Mistress."

There were many questions that floated in my head. That

was never one of them. Things were always easier when I was on my knees. Even when I had to move or stop because discomfort started settling in... Listening was easier there. Staying calm, too. Even talking. Whether or not I needed my phone, there was just less pressure when I assumed the position. Things were clearer. Breathing took less effort. There was more oxygen, somehow.

"Kneel, then."

"Yes, Mistress."

I rushed to obey, holding my breath as I settled on the pillow Mistress had placed on the floor. She always added something soft whenever I was to kneel somewhere.

Mistress sat on the edge of the couch, close enough I could probably count the pores in Her toned thighs, but not close enough I could touch. She rested Her elbows on Her knees, leaning forward. Most people who hadn't played a lot with Her would feel intimidated. My heart started thudding faster, too. But this was Mistress Erika. No amount of leering was going to make me feel unsafe around Her.

"You already do this, so I don't presume it will be hard, but as my property, you are only to come when you have my explicit permission to do so."

My breath hitched. I couldn't squeeze my thighs together without the aloe sticking, but the urge was there. "Yes, Mistress."

"Good." The simple word washed through my body before I realized it needed cleansing. Objectively, I knew all these reactions were about the novelty of the relationship, of adding this new layer to what we were doing. Secretly, I nurtured the feeling that I'd always react like this to Her. It was the trust I had in Her that She'd always bring this out of me. "It's not the only thing."

Of course not.

I preened, waiting. I'd been waiting all this time—all my

adult life, really—for more rules, more structure. More ways in which the world around me could make sense.

Mistress Erika tucked two fingers under my chin, forcing my gaze up.

I didn't blink. I couldn't.

"I want you to have at least an hour of speech restriction every day," She said. There was no wavering, no hesitance in Her words. "Before heading up to bed, after all chores are done, you'll be a perfect object for me."

I breathed out. "Yes, Mistress."

My eyes fluttered closed. This was why I trusted Her, why I didn't care about Her concerns that we were going too fast. Before I could question anything, She stood right there, giving me exactly what I wanted.

I had so many fantasies about what She'd described, it was hard not to squirm, not to beg Her to start right now or moan out loud. Being quiet was more of a challenge than it usually was.

I welcomed it. I welcomed all the feelings and sensations that came from sharing space with Her. Being with Her felt both exhilaratingly new and as familiar as breathing. I supposed it was both things.

"One day, being an object will mean holding a tabletop position and letting me rest my feet on your back." Mistress continued talking. I let myself get drunk with every word as I pictured the scenario She described. "On a different day, it will mean standing still while I test a new toy on you."

I nodded. I didn't know if She was waiting for input right this second. I didn't know if She wanted me to verbalize what I was thinking. It didn't matter. I wanted it. Objectification, for me, wasn't a purely sexual kink. Heat built down in my belly as I thought of being used as a toy tester, as I stood there being degraded to the point where I didn't feel human. But I got the same reaction from picturing myself as a table for Mistress to rest on, or a coat hanger, or anything that put me in the background as a mere tool to serve and bring comfort of any kind.

It was the spark that made me feel alive, that made me feel truly wanted. Needed.

Loved.

"What do you think about that, slut?"

I whimpered. Being called a slut was nothing new. Mistress had been alternating between slut and pet for as long as we'd been playing together. Pet was reserved for nonsexual things or moments when She wanted to make it clear there was no intent to humiliate. Slut was used way more often.

Surely, that would mean I had no reason to react as strongly as I did to it. I should be desensitized to the word, but I wasn't. Every time, my breath caught and my heart started beating faster, my whole body on alert.

My throat felt dry when I parted my lips. There was a question to answer, but the words wouldn't move past my throat.

I coughed, then blushed. I'd meant to clear my throat—subtly—but it must've gone down the wrong pipe.

"I want that more than anything." My voice came out wrong.

Raspy.

Mistress Erika tilted Her head to the side. Her eyes were narrowed, watching. "Are you okay?"

"Yes." This time, I sounded stronger. I closed my eyes for a second. I wasn't a believer, but I still sent my thanks to the universe for it. "Yes, Mistress."

"An hour is a long time," She pointed out.

Another time, maybe I would've responded more playfully. I would've squinted my eyes and teased that it sounded like She wanted to discourage me. Or maybe that was how another sub would've responded, someone who hadn't dreamed about this for years. Someone who didn't fantasize about giving up all control and power.

"I'm aware, Mistress."

I'd acted as a table for Her before, in the club. I'd been told to stay quiet and still while She used a toy on me before. I didn't think it had lasted an hour, and I didn't know that I could do it right away. But I knew Mistress was more aware of my limits than She was of Hers. If She said I could do an hour, then I would let Her guide me to take that hour. It was as simple as that.

"Good." Her eyes glinted as her gaze darted across my face. There had to be something else. I kept my position on my knees as I waited to hear what it would be. "I also want you to learn about Ethiopian cuisine."

"Yes, Mistress." It didn't take a lot to nod, but there were things I wanted to say about it.

I just…

"Phone, slut."

Right.

I blinked. Where was my phone? Panic seized me for a second. I twisted my fingers. One thing I didn't lose awareness of was where my phone was—or whatever I was using as an aid to share what I was needing to say but couldn't voice out loud.

The device appeared in front of me before the building panic could escalate.

Mistress.

I breathed out. It must've been on the couch, but that wasn't where my focus lay.

Mistress had anticipated me before I could make my panic known. She'd read me perfectly. Again.

"Thank you, Mistress."

There was no response, but Her lips tilted up into a soft smile when I grabbed the phone from Her hands.

We had classes on different international cuisines in school, but it was all French, Italian, Japanese... I wrote a letter complaining about the lack of courses on African and Southwest Asian cuisine, but they ignored it.

But I found an online bootcamp. I signed up for it, but I'm on the waiting list. They only run it once a year.

Mistress frowned for a second while She read. I chewed on my lip. I knew it wasn't perfect, that I should have—and could have—done more. There were probably more resources that I hadn't found. I could dig deeper—or I could've insisted when my letter was ignored.

"Send me the link to the bootcamp," She said. "The couple next door runs an Ethiopian restaurant. I take Kara there sometimes. Maybe they can teach you some things, too."

I squirmed. Meeting new people always brought anxiety. It was rare that I made a good impression. Even when my voice didn't get in the way, I never felt like I knew how to approach people. I didn't know what was too much, or too little. I didn't think I got it right.

"Yes, Mistress."

Taking things one step at a time was important. In this case, the first step was sending the link to the bootcamp. I could do that with no problem. I'd deal with meeting Mistress's neighbors when She decided to make it happen.

I really wanted to learn more international cuisines, and

learning from the source was always best. If I felt self-conscious about it, I could get past it.

"May I ask you something?"

"You may."

"Two things, actually."

I blurted out the words before the thought fully formed.

Mistress laughed. "Go ahead, pet."

She ran a finger across my cheekbone as She spoke. The soft touch made me shiver.

"Are you…" I licked my lips. There was an uncomfortable combination of not having the words ready and beating myself up over not knowing something that felt too… basic. It was moments like these when it really dawned on me that I didn't know much about Mistress outside of the image She portrayed within the walls of Plumas. "Is Ethiopian culture a big part of your life?"

I should research holidays, and traditions, and… more. Probably.

"No." Mistress shook Her head before I could spiral into creating more lists of things to do in my head. "I was adopted as a toddler by white parents who didn't care too much about my roots. But food is one of the few comforts I let myself indulge in. I can't say I connect a lot with other aspects, but eating fir fir feels like reclaiming something, and like… kicking the system that wanted to distort my identity."

I nodded. For once, the lack of words felt like the most fitting response. There wasn't much I could say anyway. I'd known Mistress Erika was adopted, but that was all I'd known. She'd never invited follow-up questions while at the club, and it had felt strange to text Her with my questions.

Invasive.

Mistress sighed after a few seconds passed. "What was your other question, Eli?"

I chewed on my lip. I couldn't tell for certain if the added weight to Her tone was due to my silence or simply the topic of conversation.

I couldn't remember what it was that I'd meant to ask, but it hit me a moment later. It almost felt silly now, but...

"Can we add a time to decompress?" I cleared my throat. This time, my throat worked properly. No embarrassing coughing anywhere to be found. "In bed, maybe, we could... talk before sleeping? Or text."

Mistress watched me. Her features changed, softened. Her hold on me shifted, too. "We absolutely can. In fact, we're starting right now."

If I wasn't kneeling, my knees would've probably buckled.

It was a silly thing to get emotional over, in the grand scheme of things. The fact was clearly not stopping me.

Mistress helped me up easily. I followed Her blindly. It was now that I realized I was still only wearing boxers. I paused for a second, expecting the itch, the discomfort that came from being exposed like this with nothing to distract me.

It didn't come.

I didn't question it or ask for the hoodie back.

I just followed Mistress upstairs and let Her handle me before She had me tucked in bed beside Her.

"Are you upset with me?"

The question was easier to voice in the darkness, under the safety of the soft blankets.

"Why would I be upset with you?"

I swallowed. "I didn't know about the food or—"

Mistress's sigh stopped me. It didn't sound like back in the living room. "I'm not going to be your teacher for all things Black, Eli, but you can't know about things I don't share willingly."

I chewed on my lip. I supposed that was true. International adoption came with a lot of trauma—that, I knew—but some parents made more of an effort to keep the adoptee connected to their country. I couldn't have known Mistress's parents hadn't been like that.

It didn't feel like enough to completely excuse my lack of knowledge, but… it would have to do for now.

I tried to shake the discomfort away. Burrowing closer to Mistress helped.

"Do you think León would pierce me?"

Maybe there was something to that thing Sergio talked about. He went off about how he lost even more of his filters after a scene, and he blurted out all kinds of things during aftercare or while he was coming out of Little space. Both things had always felt like foreign concepts.

Before now, apparently.

Mistress snorted. "The guy responsible for all of his sub's piercings? I think he'd be offended if you didn't at least ask."

That made sense, I supposed.

"Danny said he could pick me up to hang out at their cabin," I explained. I didn't remember if I'd told Mistress yet. "I'll ask him then."

"Good."

It was good.

I felt good.

14

ERIKA

Sometimes, it's strange. i feel like i know you better than anyone else out there, and i take pride in that knowledge, even if i know it's not... great. But other times, you say something, or i ask you something, and i realize there is so much i don't know about you, and i don't know what to do for the rest of the day.

Then i realize that i don't hate it. i feel bad, depending on what it is, but it makes me... happy, that there is so much more to learn, and that you're letting me do it.

Every new thing i learn brings me more peace. It's not the exact type of peace that comes from serving or following your rules and our new routines, but it's close enough. i worship it regardless, and i crave more of it.

– eli

"So. What am I doing here?" I sat back on one of the few actual leather chairs in the common area of the club.

It didn't squeak, thankfully. Some squeaking was inevitable with these types of chairs, but it grated on my nerves, regardless. The last thing I needed was something else darkening my mood.

It had been a good day. It was supposed to be a good day. I'd gotten in the ring with Abel while the gym stood empty during most people's lunch break, Eli had put together the best sushi I'd ever had, and I'd officially welcomed it as the app's moderator. Supposedly, I should've had less on my plate.

Instead, I came to the club to find issues with one of our suppliers, which meant a bunch of phone calls and trying to find an alternative that would restock the bar in time. And now this.

I'd been on my way to the car. After all the calls back and forth, all my interest in spending any amount of time at Plumas had vanished for the day. Others were here, and there were enough DMs around that I didn't need to be here—or that's what I would've assumed.

Clearly, I was missing something, which in turn, only made my annoyance grow.

I tamped it down, but it was a challenge.

"The sub insisted," Tony said. There was a certain derision to his tone. For once, I could ignore it. I'd be annoyed, too. "I explained that he was supposed to go to a DM when he had an issue, and you weren't on DM duty today."

I fought the urge to scrub a hand down my face and not show any of what I was actually feeling. "Who's the sub?"

Tony hadn't given me a name. He just said a newbie had freaked out during a shibari scene. It happened more often than people would think. Shibari, and rope bondage in general, was more demanding than one would expect.

"Everest."

Fuck.

Now I scrubbed a hand down my face.

He was sweet. I'd vetted him a few months ago. Sergio had been hanging out with him if I remembered correctly. Sergio was the type to take everyone under his wing.

Danny had been roped in, too, but I couldn't say I'd seen him around much.

"Where is he?"

"I put him in your office."

"All right."

Back to the office, then. I really liked the space more when Eli was acting as decoration there. Alas, I'd left Eli at home so it could start going through the online requests in the app —and because the plan had been to deal with the provider mess, not to get distracted with play.

"Wait."

Tony grabbed me by the elbow. It took everything in me not to shove him into the nearest wall. Ever since Sergio had come clean about their history—Tony having taken advantage of his position as Sergio's TA, all while in the closet and being the older brother of Sergio's high school bully—I couldn't say I found it easy to conceal my... untoward feelings toward the man. I'd been sympathetic when he'd been outed in a local newspaper, but the abuse of power took precedence.

"Hands off."

"Right. Sorry." He raised both palms in the air. It was hard not to roll my eyes. "What do you want to do about the riggers?"

I did a double take. I had no details whatsoever about the situation, and I was supposed to... what, exactly?

Did I read minds now? See the future?

"Keep an eye on them. I'm going to talk with Everest first."

For all I knew, the riggers had done nothing. Even someone who'd made as many questionable choices as Tony would have noticed if someone was ignoring a safeword or skipping a boundary.

Thankfully, he didn't fight that and just gave me a nod.

I went down the hallway and up the stairs to the room I used as my office. If it had been me on the floor, I would've left Everest with either another DM or a sub he was friends with, but there was nothing to do about it now.

Everest sat on the small couch that was tucked against the wall. His knees were to his chest, but he stood up the second I opened the door.

"Ma'am." He breathed out the word, not in reverence like Eli would, but in relief.

The heartbreaking kind.

"Can I get you anything?"

"No." He shook his head right away. "Tony made me drink some water."

That was a point in the man's favor, I supposed. "All right. Can you fill me in on what happened?"

Everest didn't react right away. I tried to examine his body for visible signs of… anything, but there was nothing amiss. He wore black briefs and a mesh sleeveless shirt, and he had a few marks of the rope, but nothing too irritated or dark in shade. His dirty blond hair looked as perfectly coiffed as I always saw it.

He was shaking, though, from head to toe.

Hadn't Tony offered him a blanket? I didn't want to ask before he answered. Crowding people was not my style—definitely not when they were already overwhelmed.

"They recognized me."

Fuck.

Okay.

"We talked about that possibility." Back when I was vetting him, I hadn't recognized him, but he was the one who brought up that concern. "What happened, exactly?"

"I know, we did, but—" Everest cut himself off, gulping for breath. Before he could continue, I helped him back to the couch and squatted down in front of him. His next breath was smoother. "I was tied up, and th-they said... They taunted me about— They..."

"Had they given any indication that they knew who you were when you were negotiating the scene?"

I didn't know that the exact words the men said were as important as the answer to the question.

"No." Everest didn't even need a second before he answered. His eyes were on me, unwavering, lips pursed. "We talked online. I can show you the chat. My profile doesn't say anything about my last name."

I nodded. Yeah, he had one of those profiles with a vague handle and even more vague pictures.

"Do you know if they're members, or just online?"

Everest swallowed. "They said they were waiting to be vetted, but you said I could invite someone as a member."

"You can," I hedged, "but if they're not official members, it's more... complicated."

As guests, they hadn't signed anything that ensured people's privacy. Members could invite someone, but it fell under their responsibility if shit happened because of it. Shit like someone leaking another person's name or their... proclivities. The society we were a part of still used someone's sex life as an excuse to discriminate, fire, or worse.

"I know, I'm responsible, I just..." Everest swallowed again. He curled his arms around his stomach. "I'm sorry."

"I'll talk to them." Even if there were no papers signed,

one thing was clear. "It doesn't matter whether or not you're recognizable. You never consented to having your identity used as part of the scene. That's a clear breach in my book."

Everest nodded. "I froze. I just... I didn't know what to do. I don't know what to do. If it gets out—"

"I'll see what I can do about it." There wasn't a lot I could promise, which was why I left it at that. "In the meantime, stick to vetted members, okay? There are no guarantees you won't have bad scenes, but I'll be able to exert more pressure on members."

At the very least, the vague threat pulled a smile out of the boy. "Yeah. I'll just hang out with Sergio and Danny."

Sounded good to me, at least while he worked through the identity issues. That brought another question, however. "Do those two know who you are?"

Everest looked down. It was all the response I needed. "No, I... When we go out, my bodyguards keep their distance, and I... I like the sense of normalcy."

It wasn't a position I envied, that was for sure, but I felt compelled to push. "Do you value that sense of normalcy more than you do their friendship?"

"Wh-what do you mean?"

"I won't judge your answer." I really wouldn't. "But I wouldn't like you to be caught off guard if one of them runs into an article about you, feels betrayed, and shit hits the fan."

His eyes widened before a frown settled on his face. I didn't get the impression that he'd considered the possibility. To be fair, neither was the type to read the kind of yellow magazines where his face might show up, but social media was there, and the algorithms worked in unpredictable ways.

"They won't hate me, right? When I tell them?"

"No." As annoying as they both could be in their own ways, they were part of my inner circle, and there was no one

I trusted more than a member of my inner circle. "Sergio will come up with the wildest questions. Danny will tease you a bit. That's it."

Everest nodded to himself. "I can handle that."

"Good." I palmed my thighs before standing up. "Stay here as long as you need, okay? And text me later if you need anything. I'll send Tony your way."

"Thanks." Everest still looked like he needed a minute to compose himself, but the strain in his muscles that had been there when I walked in had vanished. I'd take my wins where I could. "And I'm sorry. Master Tony said you weren't on duty today and he could help with whatever it was, but I didn't want to have to explain everything and deal with... You know."

I forced the gentlest smile I could muster. "It's all right, Everest."

"I prefer Ev, actually." He cleared his throat, a blush coming to his cheeks. "It's a thing Sergio's trying out."

Of course it was Sergio's doing. "Ev, then."

Huh. I wondered if I could use his name as an excuse for Abel to drop that *Er* nickname. Surely, it would get confusing with the two of us.

ELI WAS RIGHT THERE when I finally made it back to the duplex. On its knees, in perfect position. It was my own knees that buckled at the sight. Today was supposed to be a good day. The bad shit had been fixed—hopefully. I should be okay. I shouldn't be picturing myself collapsing.

"Mistress?"

Fuck.

I didn't know what was going on, but I didn't like it. Eli's voice sounded muffled, as if there was a layer between us. I blinked, trying to put the sub into focus.

It didn't work.

I really didn't like whatever was going on. My limbs suddenly felt like lead. Heavy. Uncooperative.

"Mistress?"

The voice came from closer. More alarmed, too.

15

ELI

Shit.

"Mistress?"

This time when I called Her name, Her gaze zeroed in on me. It would've been more relieving if She looked anything like Herself.

"Yeah. Sorry, pet. Need to sit down."

I frowned. There were too many questions. Questions I didn't have an answer to. Questions I didn't think I could voice out loud when Mistress looked so... ashen.

What happened at the club? She said She had to make some calls, deal with some providers that had fucked up a delivery. I could imagine that kind of thing would be stressful, but Mistress looked... beyond stressed. She looked exhausted.

I got off my knees right away. It was more brazen than what was expected of a slave, but I didn't think this was part of play. I grabbed Erika's wrist and pulled until She was walking to me. I bet when She talked about sitting down, She just meant the couch, but it was late, and She looked like She needed to lie down more than She needed to sit down. So I made the—scary—executive decision of veering us toward Her bed.

"Where are you—"

She didn't even finish that sentence. I didn't have to spare Her a look or say a word, either.

I was acting on some sort of adrenaline, I was aware. There was no telling if I'd feel as confident in five, ten minutes, but I was taking advantage now.

Erika slumped down on the bed the second I pushed Her to it. Knees bent, She covered Her face with both hands, letting out a guttural groan.

"Fuck." It was still strange to hear Her curse. "Help me take off my clothes. Please."

Her voice broke when She said please. It came out croaked. Unnatural, almost. Maybe that was why I didn't think and just jumped to do as She said. She'd changed before leaving the club—or maybe She'd just never put on any gear since She was there for admin stuff. I didn't know. It wasn't important to ask about it now, but it was convenient that the clothes I had to take off were just joggers, a sports jacket, and one of those T-shirts that was supposed to be warm while breathable. Or something.

It was a good thing that my lack of familiarity with gyms or workouts hadn't come up at any point.

"Want me to lie on top of you?"

Weight helped. I knew it helped Her.

There was a pause. An almost imperceptible nod. I finished folding all Her clothes in record speed, leaving them at the foot of the bed, before crawling on top of Her. My own clothes were still on, but I didn't want to wait.

I'd never seen Erika down. I'd seen Her not in the mood for play or upset about something and needing to rant. I'd never seen Her... depleted. That was the word that described Her best right now.

She wrapped Her arms around the middle of my back and squeezed tight. I stayed still, letting Her get what She needed from me. Wanting Her to.

Her skin was colder than usual. Not worryingly so, but I noticed anyway. I was used to Her quiet warmth, to the way She looked intimidating to everyone else but brought me the most comfort out of anyone at the club.

"I'm sorry," She grumbled.

"Why?" The question slipped past my lips before She'd finished talking.

There was no way I could compute why She'd apologize for… whatever was going on. I just wanted to know how to help and what I was helping with. She shouldn't have to apologize for that.

"I don't… I feel like I'm crumbling down." I watched as Erika licked Her lips, as Her face twisted with… worry, confusion, distaste. So many emotions, and I didn't like any of them. "There's always something."

I frowned. When I was struggling, it helped when people asked questions. It kept me on track, helped me focus.

There was a possibility that I was wrong and proving to everyone that I was not good at this, but I always got the impression that Erika worked in the opposite way. She wouldn't do well with someone setting the pace. She would be the kind of person who would start talking on Her own, at Her own pace, with meaningful pauses that shouldn't be interrupted.

For once, staying quiet was the challenging part, but I did it. I covered as much of Her body as I could with mine, and I waited.

"I can't take care of everyone," Erika whispered. "I can't be in charge of everything. I don't even want to."

"You don't?"

Shit.

I flinched.

Erika just squeezed me to Her. She moved her hand to my lower back. It was soothing, grounding. I didn't like that it had to be, but I liked the end result, nonetheless.

"I just want to be in charge of you." Erika licked Her lips. "And everything else, but not... so fast. Not at the same time."

I wasn't sure I understood what that meant. I wanted Her to be in charge of me, too, but had I triggered something? Maybe I should've waited, like She'd wanted to. I didn't want to regret speaking up, but... had I pushed too hard?

"I don't know how I'm supposed to fix it."

What was there to fix?

I frowned, sitting up. Erika let me, Her hands shifting to my hips. "Don't."

Any other day, the way She mimicked my expression would've been amusing. "Don't what?"

"Don't." I huffed. There were too many ways to end that sentence, too many things to command Her not to do. "Let *me* fix it."

"This isn't on you," She replied right away, Her eyes crinkling at the corners.

It had been predictable, but predictable wasn't going to stop me. Just because I preferred delegating to Her most of the time didn't mean I couldn't be stubborn. I'd fielded complaints about how stubborn I could be for most of my life.

"I don't care."

For the longest seconds, Erika only watched me. I waited with bated breath. Was She going to call my bluff?

I didn't know that it was a bluff to begin with, but it felt like one. If She agreed, I wouldn't know where to start. I wasn't the one who came up with the plans to cheer up people when they were going through something. That was

Erika and the other Domms. María, too, sometimes. Or Sergio and Kara, if they were the ones who noticed first.

"Kiss me, pet."

Was that acquiescence?

I'd take it as such.

After I obeyed, of course. The simple command was one of the most rewarding to follow. My toes curled as I sneaked up the bed until my face hovered mere inches over Erika. She was the most beautiful Domme I'd ever been with. The most beautiful Domme I wanted to be with. I supported my weight on my hands before leaning down, covering Her lips with mine. I wanted to bring Her comfort. I didn't know if soft lips on Her were enough, but Her grip on my hips tightened. It wasn't a big shift, but it was enough—I noticed it.

Erika hummed against my lips, which gave me my answer —I was doing good.

There was something strange about the kind of... almost innocent... kissing. There weren't any wandering hands or the goal to move south. It wasn't a touch meant to drive anyone wild with desire. Its simplicity was staggering; it made me lose my footing, in absence of a better metaphor.

It was good, too. It turned out kissing just for the sake of it brought its own brand of satisfaction. Soon, I was inundated by Erika's scent, drowning in her essence, in the softness of her skin. I was wrapped up in an invisible blanket, in a bubble that molded to our bodies and warmed the air around us.

"I love you."

The words came as easy as breathing. They were just there, lingering between our lips, curling around that thin string of saliva keeping us tied together.

"Eli," Erika warned.

It was a warning, but it was a plea, too.

I'd never wondered what Erika would look like pleading. It had been an oversight on my part.

"I love you," I repeated. I had for the longest time. It was the only natural consequence to being around Her. "I love you."

I'd repeat it until She believed it, until the words sank in and felt as natural as saying them out loud did.

It didn't matter if my throat ended up burning, if my vocal cords gave in on me. The feeling was here, everywhere around us. It wasn't going away. Erika had to feel it, too. There was no other way, no other option.

Eventually, Erika nodded. She shifted us around until She was spooning me. I moved too much during the night, so I already knew the position wouldn't last long. It didn't matter.

Erika's lips landed on the curve of my neck. For a few seconds, She just stayed there. Still. Then She placed a kiss there, followed by another. She tightened Her arm around my waist, pulling me close to Her, until there was no room for air between us. I'd have to take my clothes off, but nothing sounded more unappealing.

"Thank you."

More of that warmth we created engulfed me. I didn't need anything other than the two of us here. I'd figure out everything else when we had to leave this cocoon, but I...

I believed in us. In this. I believed enough for the two of us. I just had to prove it to Her.

16

ELI

I usually wait until I've processed things before I talk, or write, about them. I don't like rambling for hours on end until I reach what I want to say.

But I haven't been doing things the usual way for... longer than I'm willing to admit, and I guess I'm not ready to break that just yet.

Last night was... You gave me everything I needed. More than what I thought I needed. In a way, it makes me feel less... adequate, but those are just voices in my head, the doubts that keep creeping in with statements I know to be wrong.

I just want to feel like I can give you what you need—what I want to give you, too. And I'll do it.

I'll do it.

- Erika

'd read Erika's note at least ten times. Each time, I added a new intonation, a new hidden meaning behind the words.

While I left the tofu marinating in the fridge, I remembered what Erika asked me weeks ago now, when I first came to Her apartment. She'd asked what I'd do if she dropped. I'd never seen Her or heard of Her dropping. It wasn't something I'd spent a long time thinking about.

I wondered if a part of Her had known. Or if it was more common than She let others believe.

There were too many questions I didn't have an answer for.

I only hesitated for a few seconds before I grabbed my phone. Back when She'd asked, I'd answered, and part of that answer had involved reaching out to others. Erika had seemed pleased with it, so it was only right that I kept my word.

ELI

> can i talk to you, Ma'am?
>
> it's about Mistress Erika

MÓNICA

Is everything all right?

ELI

> i think, no, i know She's struggling
>
> i am helping, but i think talking with you would help

MÓNICA

Did anything happen?

ELI

> no
>
> well, i don't know

JUST ONE RULE

> i think She's dropping
>
> i tried to keep Her from going to the gym today, but She wouldn't bulge

MÓNICA

Okay

I already promised I'd visit my mother during my lunch break, but I'll drop by your place after work

Do you need me to grab anything?

ELI

> you know Her as well as i do, Ma'am

They weren't words I said freely. If I'd texted anyone else, even if they'd also been part of the club from the beginning, I wouldn't have. Mónica was the exception.

I didn't need to have spent a lot of time with Mónica and Erika outside of the club to know they really were close. Their friendship might not be as loud as Sergio and Kara's, but it was there, clear in every interaction.

I knew Erika relied on Mónica, too. They had each other's backs.

MÓNICA

You're sweet

Do you know if Abel is working at the gym today?

ELI

> i can ask Sergio

I was friends with Sergio's Daddy on the club's app, but I didn't have his number, and I knew he didn't use the app a lot, so I doubted he would while he was at the gym. Sergio playfully complained about it often.

> MÓNICA
>
> Okay
>
> Erika tends to push herself when she's working through something, so just tell him to keep an eye on her

> ELI
>
> yes, Ma'am

Not surprisingly, Sergio was too happy to text the second I asked him about his Daddy. By texting, I meant he sent a million crying emojis about being abandoned at home with no one to pester and the unfairness of it all. He did text Abel when I told him about Erika, so he was forgiven for all the dramatics.

"MISTRESS?"

I hesitated when I called for Her. I hated it. I'd spent most of the day going back and forth. How was I meant to behave? I didn't know anything about Mistress Erika when She dropped. Some Domms wanted nothing to do with honorifics or protocols when they weren't feeling their best. Others still wanted some semblance of a routine.

In the end, I'd told myself I'd try to follow the protocol and go from Her reactions to it. Mónica would be here soon, too, and I was counting on her helping. It didn't take away from the nerves buzzing through my skin, though.

Mistress was halfway through taking off Her coat when She noticed me. I'd just seen Her that morning, but She looked tired. More so than when I'd kissed Her goodbye hours ago.

I frowned. I'd known it was a bad idea that She went to work, but She'd dismissed it. She'd said taking a day off wasn't an option when She ran the place. I understood—I supposed I didn't have another choice—but I should've fought Her more on it. Abel could put more hours in if She asked him, or they could call in more of the part-time trainers Mistress had on payroll, or... something.

Then again, the idea popped into my head that She'd gone because She'd needed the space. There weren't many solutions I could offer to that particular dilemma.

It was disconcerting, in a way.

"How have you been, pet?"

I swallowed. Mistress stood closer after She'd hung up Her coat and got out of Her sneakers. She moved Her hand to my jaw when I didn't answer right away. Concern began to mar Her features.

Shit.

My heart beat faster. Her concern should prompt me to give an answer, to do... something. It paralyzed me, instead.

The buzz of the intercom was my saving grace. I hated that it was.

"Are we expecting someone?"

"Mónica." I cleared my throat. "She said she was dropping by."

It wasn't the best explanation, but it would have to do.

Mistress didn't question it. She just moved to the intercom and buzzed Her friend in.

But then She was back on me. "What do you need, Eli?"

I gulped. "I don't know."

The words grated against my throat. My eyes smarted. I'd told myself I was going to keep it together. I had to. It wasn't fair on Mistress if I didn't. I was supposed to show Her that I could do this, that we could be equals and I could hold Her weight when the situation called for it. Otherwise, it would mean She'd been right, and it had been irresponsible of me to ask for more than what we'd already had.

No.

I shook that thought off. It was just my head, playing tricks. I was too used to people walking on eggshells around me and living with the knowledge that there were expectations set on me. Those expectations weren't like Mistress's expectations to follow the rules and protocols we'd negotiated. They were stifling—either condescending in their low requirements, or the kind that only existed to bathe me in shame when I disappointed the people holding them.

So I'd learned to question everyone and everything, to believe that things were on me to fix, because only then did I surpass those expectations. Only then could I breathe.

Mistress wasn't like that. She wasn't going to blame me or be disappointed in me. The point of turning everything into rules, routines, and protocols was to get rid of all those hidden meanings, all those unspoken rules and norms.

Mistress didn't answer. She didn't scold me for not knowing or furrow Her brows while questioning everything She'd ever thought about me. But She kissed me. It was short —a graze of lips that lingered so close Her breath teased my skin.

I melted against Her hold, and She was there to catch me.

I didn't have to wonder about anything else. I just had to stay in Her arms, to kiss Her back, to let Her take as much of the lead as She wanted to.

The doorbell rang. The shock pulled us apart. I didn't care. I'd gotten all I needed.

"Thank you, Mistress."

A frown etched in Her features. I knew She probably wanted to ask, but I'd already walked past Her so I could open the door.

Mónica greeted me with a quick hug before taking off her shoes and lining them next to Mistress Erika's. I helped hang her coat next. It wasn't discussed, but I didn't think it needed to be.

"Thank you, Eli."

I smiled.

Mónica was a soft Domme through and through, a combination of a leather Domme who enjoyed seeing what a sub could handle for her and a Mommy Domme who didn't like being referred to as a Mommy, even though Littles were her Achilles' heel. Even before Kara arrived at the club, everyone knew Mónica was weak to a Little's puppy eyes. That tidbit of knowledge had been exploited plenty of times, probably without her knowing.

Nothing about being Mistress's slave meant I had to come clean about the shenanigans the other subs at the club got into.

It was for the better.

"Any of you hungry?" Mónica asked after giving Mistress a not-so-subtle glance over.

"You're annoying," Mistress grumbled. "Eli has cooked."

I had. Mónica hadn't said anything about bringing food. She was holding a plastic bag, but I couldn't see any takeout containers or any logos from any of the restaurants we used to order from.

Mónica winked when she turned toward me. She was even more playful ever since she'd gotten together with Kara. I should probably text her Little more. It was hard to keep track of everything, but Kara was nice. More sunshine than I thought when she first joined the club. It was hard not to smile around her.

"On a scale of one to ten, how much would you hate me if I take you both out for an early dinner?"

I frowned. I couldn't say I was the biggest fan of plans changing, but the food would keep. It wasn't something that needed to be eaten fresh. I could plop the baking dish in the fridge and reheat it in the oven tomorrow.

"I don't hate you, Ma'am."

But I'd text her to let her know next time I'd appreciate a warning.

I didn't think she'd done it on purpose. Mónica had a demanding job that kept her busy. She might not have had time to come up with a plan until she was driving here. It wasn't fair to hold it against her.

"Good." Mistress glowered behind her while Mónica grinned. "I brought ice cream, too. Kara's contribution."

Of course.

Kara worked as Mónica's secretary. Even if Mónica hadn't had a lot of free time, she would've let Kara know. Or maybe Kara just heard about it because Sergio texted her. The two of them were real gossips, and news traveled fast whenever something happened with one of the club members.

"I'll put it in the freezer, Ma'am."

It would give me something to do because I'd started to fidget, and it would give Mónica a minute with Mistress.

The Domme didn't think anything weird about my offer. She just handed me the plastic bag. I pretended not to see Mistress's eye roll. It was kind of endearing. I wouldn't have said Mistress had a grumpy side to Her, but that was the only way I could describe Her attitude right now.

Or like a prickly cat.

Huh.

I wondered how Mistress felt about pets.

Then again, that was probably a question better saved for… a six-month anniversary. That seemed a reasonable timeline.

Whatever.

The ice cream tub was lemon sorbet. I would've expected something sweeter coming from Kara. Both Mistress and I preferred tarter flavors, so it was not a complaint.

I had to remember that the people at the club knew us, and they cared. Just because not even one of my relatives would've taken my taste into consideration when gifting me something didn't mean that was the right thing. People who cared proved that they did.

When I walked back to the entrance, Mistress and Mónica were whispering among themselves. Mónica nudged Her shoulder. Mistress did more of that scowling.

It really was sweet—and that was how I knew I was done for.

"Where are we going, Ma'am?"

"There's a new Vietnamese restaurant that opened near my place," Mónica answered promptly. "You both can change while I text Kara to assure her no one is dying."

Oh. Right.

I glanced down.

Mistress didn't care about dress codes when we were at home, so I just wore comfortable clothes I stole from Her wardrobe. More deliveries kept arriving with the things I'd asked of Her, clothes and random necessities—as Mistress called them—but I still preferred grabbing Her old clothes. Mistress just teased me about it from time to time, but She hadn't said it was against the rules. Everyone knew that meant it wasn't.

"Come on, pet."

Mistress pretended to be resigned to it, but I knew she liked Vietnamese food from one of our talks in bed, and I was too excited about the prospect of going out with Her to care.

It wasn't that I hadn't left the house since I'd arrived or that we hadn't gone out together. But I wasn't so out of it not to acknowledge that, if up to my own devices, I *was* a homebody.

Mistress was, too, in a different way.

Regardless. Going out was exciting, and I wasn't going to let those pesky, vulnerable thoughts get in the way of enjoying the outing.

"Yes, Mistress."

17

ERIKA

"So, what's going on with you?"

I scowled. I knew I was doing it, and I knew it was immature.

I didn't care.

"Can you at least let me enjoy my soup?"

I hadn't had pho in forever. I didn't know that I had the stomach to fully enjoy it, but that was apparently not going to keep me from making my protest clear.

"I let you enjoy your spring rolls," Mónica pointed out. She had that look on her face, the one I was sure she'd perfected every time she'd showed her litter of brothers how much smarter she was. It was annoying. "Now speak."

I huffed.

The restaurant was nicely decorated in lighter tones of sage green. Most importantly, it was almost empty. There were only two other tables, and they were more than a safe distance for us to talk without risk of anyone eavesdropping. There was no shame in any of the ways we engaged, but it was a concern, nonetheless.

"Did you hear anything about Ev?" I asked her instead.

To be fair, it was a valid concern. I'd made a note to text him later, but that note hadn't considered that I'd be roped into an intervention.

"The new guy?" Mónica frowned.

She'd tied up her hair in a bun, showing the undercut beneath. It reminded me I still needed to call to get an appointment for my own hair.

How long had I been thinking that?

I wasn't the kind of person who procrastinated on scheduling plans or left things for the last minute. The mere idea sent shivers up my spine.

The bad kind.

"Yeah." I cleared my throat as I leaned against the backrest of the bamboo chair. "He had a bad scene last night."

Mónica straightened in her seat, spoon forgotten. "How bad?"

"Breach of privacy bad."

I had both of them eyeing me now. Right. With no background, that made no sense to them. I groaned into my palms. This wasn't me. I didn't slip like this.

Eli nudged my side.

I glanced in its direction to see it was holding its phone to me, screen unlocked.

if you need to discuss something i'm not supposed to hear, i can excuse myself to the bathroom, Mistress

I shook my head right away. If anything, Eli needed to hear it now that it was in charge of moderating the app. I doubted the riggers from last night would say a word online —or offline. I hadn't gotten that vibe from them when I'd spoken to them before leaving the club. But someone else might recognize Ev, and they might comment something online even if they were a member because they thought the app was a safe space.

"Not a word to Kara," I warned Mónica.

Sergio *might* tell her, depending on how Ev framed the talk with him, but I couldn't extinguish every single flame.

"Sure."

It wasn't that I didn't trust Mónica. I did. I was just very aware that talking about this was one hundred percent not my place.

"Ev is an... important public figure." It was the most I could compromise. "If it came out that he was a member of a kink club? It would get messy."

Mónica's eyebrow arched. "Okay... All members sign that version of an NDA Tony wrote up."

"He was playing with some guys he met through the app." I sighed, leaning back. "Not vetted members."

"Fuck."

"Yeah." I turned toward Eli. "I'm going to need you to set an alert or something with his name and cut off every conversation that has to do with his identity."

"Yes, Mistress."

Eli's eyes shone with concern, but there was no hesitation as it nodded.

"That's not the only thing, is it?" Mónica asked.

"Uh?"

Mónica looked way too confident as she sat back. "Are you really going to bullshit me?"

I hated it, but I glanced to Eli. There were no questions, no need for a command. Eli just stood up and headed toward the restrooms. My stomach churned at the sight.

The idea that a sub shouldn't be aware of their Domm's struggles was one I never agreed with. I hadn't changed my mind there. I knew I had to talk to Eli, to explain myself and everything that was going on.

But I needed to make sense of it first, and I didn't want anyone—let alone Eli—to have to second-guess the jumbling thoughts that kept running through my head.

"Well?" Mónica had her eyebrow quirked up. She had things to say about Eli leaving. Both of us were aware. "What's going on with you?"

"I don't even know." I huffed. "I don't know what I'm doing."

"Miss *I have ten plans running simultaneously at any given time?*"

I scowled. "Don't tease me."

"Start making sense, then."

Mónica's words held a small degree of mockery, but her expression had sobered. It was what we did. I wasn't going to hold the teasing against her, but it was good to know I didn't need to spell everything out.

"It's... Eli. María. Sergio. Tony. Now Ev. The providers. The gym. My hair. The fucking app with all the new online members that refuse to show their faces. It's..." I clenched my fists. It was already more than I'd planned to say out loud, and yet, I got the feeling that I'd barely scratched the surface. "Everything's blowing up, or about to."

"Okay, let's take it one thing at a time. Start with Eli and go from there."

I exhaled. "Eli's literally just been kicked out by the only relative it had left. No matter how much I spin it, it's completely dependent on me. It has basically nothing to its name other than its phone. I don't know how to make it so I'm not quite literally abusing it."

"Wow." Mónica raised a hand. "Maybe we don't jump to abuse right off the bat?"

I glared. Was it petty?

Maybe.

"Right now, if Eli wanted to end shit with me, it literally wouldn't be able to."

"Eli also looks and sounds the most settled I've seen them in probably years," Mónica pointed out. "But what are we? Chopped liver? If Eli wanted to end things with you, at any point, and let's say that they had no chance of buying or renting or sharing a place, don't you think at least one of us would let them in for as long as they needed?"

"You don't know that."

Those were all nice words, but it wasn't as simple.

"Do you want it in writing? Because I'll do it."

Surely, I didn't just roll my eyes because I was in a weird mood. "Don't be ridiculous."

"Pot, meet kettle."

Ugh.

Mónica could be infuriating. Had I mentioned that in the last week? She needed constant reminders or it got to her head.

"What about everyone else?"

I sighed. Where did I start? "María is hurt because I never got to talk to her before things exploded, Tony has been outed and has no support whatsoever and is still more of an asshole than anyone should be comfortable with. Sergio is not going to fucking therapy to work through the stuff that happened with Tony, which means there's no reparation there on sight. And there's just *always* something going on. Everywhere."

Mónica hummed. "And your hair?"

"Need an appointment," I grumbled.

"Okay. Grab your phone and set it up, then."

"Huh?"

"Can't you book it online?"

"Yes?"

I was sure I could. I'd never tried to do it. Did that make me a geriatric millennial? Was that a thing in my mid-thirties?

"So, do it, and we'll address your control freak tendencies later."

"I'm not a control freak."

"You one hundred percent are." Mónica grinned way too widely as she said that. "While you're at it, text your slave to come back here."

I squinted my eyes. Mónica had never referred to Eli as my slave. It was pretty clear that she'd just done that now purposefully.

"I hate you."

I did both of the things she said.

"You're a good Domme, Erika, and you don't need me to tell you that." Mónica sighed before glancing toward the restrooms. Eli was just emerging from the door to the gender neutral one. "You are the most careful Domme I've met, and Eli can tell when shit is wrong, and they're vocal about it."

"I don't know what you mean by that."

"Mean by what?" Eli sat back down next to me, only offering Mónica a quick smile before doing it.

"Isn't your Mistress the most thoughtful and careful when discussing dynamics with you?" Mónica used her sweetest voice.

"Now you're pushing it."

Eli just blinked. "But you are."

"I…"

I had no idea what I was going to say. Thankfully—for me —the owner of the restaurant chose that moment to walk past our table to greet someone at the entrance. It wasn't long enough of a respite, but it was better than nothing.

"Mistress," Eli whispered, "I don't know what… happened. But you aren't failing or doing anything wrong."

"And you'd tell her if she was, right, Eli?"

"You really need to take a step back."

"Nuh uh. I let you do things your way with Kara. And Abel, really. So now you deal with me doing things my way."

"You really *are* annoying."

The fact that all the ribbing and getting me to book an appointment for my hair was improving my mood significantly was beside the point. Well, it wasn't, and I'd thank her later. Right now, though, I was trying to remember why going out with Mónica had sounded like a good idea. At least at home I could boss Eli around and be distracted by it.

But no. Mónica had to be a voice of reason here.

Sure, I'd probably needed the change of scenery.

It was irrelevant.

"You'll live."

Eli's fingers wrapped around my wrist. It was shocking enough to jolt me out of my thoughts. It looked adorable in the oversized fluffy hoodie it had on. The cat ears were pulled back, but it still looked… sweet.

Not as Little-like or vulnerable as I'd thought when I got the link to it.

Eli did look squeezable.

"I'm a good judge of character, Mistress." Eli held my gaze while it spoke. A part of me wanted to snap a protest, but there was just… none. Eli *was* a good judge of character. "You are the only Mistress I'd trust with a TPE arrangement."

I swallowed, a knot in my throat making an uncomfortable appearance I could've done without. Eli looked sincere. Two months ago, I wouldn't have doubted it. I did the work. I was confident in my skill. I could have a 24/7 dynamic, and I could hold the weight of responsibility that came from a power exchange. I thrived on it. Dominating someone was the thing that energized me, the thing that brought everything into sharper focus.

Maybe that was part of the problem?

I'd played harder with Eli before it had triggered the alarms at the gym. I hadn't played with anyone else at the club, either.

But doing that didn't exactly feel right, not when I was questioning that skill and how to manage that weight on my shoulders.

Fuck.

Maybe I really was biting off more than I could chew.

"If I tell you people's impending drama isn't your business, you're just going to ignore me, aren't you?" Mónica blazed on, completely bypassing Eli's words.

"It is my business."

They were my friends. My community. I wasn't about to apologize for caring and not wanting them to go through hell.

"You can care about people without making it blur absolutely everything else." Mónica glanced up at the wallpapered ceiling. She wasn't looking, but I scowled regardless. My caring didn't blur anything else—usually. Just because I was clearly over my head right now didn't negate that fact. I kind of resented the assumption that it did. I knew what I was doing. "María has attachment issues to work through, regardless of your role in enabling her. Ev has his own issues if he's putting himself in clearly dangerous situations while he isn't ready to face the possible consequences. Sergio is a full-fledged adult and will work through his trauma however he sees fit. And yeah, I sympathize with how Tony was outed, but it doesn't change the fact that he still is one of the Doms I trust the least in the club. He built that rep, not you, or his past with Sergio, or anything else."

"So what? You don't feel like you owe at least trying to give him some kind of space?"

Mónica pursed her lips together for a couple of seconds. I knew what she was going to say before she did. "Not really."

To my left, Eli frowned. "I don't mind Tony."

"Don't get me wrong, I don't hate the guy." Mónica shrugged. "If he comes to me and apologizes for every comment and look he's made in the last... couple of years, and I can see he's actually working on himself, I'll be more than happy to be in his corner. Until then..."

Another shrug.

"He is working on himself," I said. I didn't know if it was something else I shouldn't be disclosing, but it felt relevant to. "I gave him some reading material, and he's discussed it with me a few times."

I understood what Mónica was saying. A part of me I'd compartmentalized felt guilty the few times I met up with Tony. In a way, it felt like I was betraying Sergio and the rest of the group. But I couldn't stand around and not offer some kind of support. Tony might have managed to keep his job, but he'd lost his family. His subs. His friends.

I knew what that felt like.

"Reading material?" Mónica cocked her head to the side. "Isn't that what you did as a pro Domme?"

I snorted. Mónica was the person I vented with after a session or after I got a message from a sub who clearly didn't know who he was talking to.

"I never said I was going to coddle him."

The idea of coddling him, or anyone else for that matter, made me shiver.

Maybe Eli.

Huh.

Picturing it didn't come easily to me. I supposed, if I had to, I wouldn't hate it.

I wouldn't love it, either, or want to make it a regular, everyday thing.

"Fair enough." Mónica paused for a second to check her phone. It could be Kara, but based on the frown that appeared, I'd wager it was either one of her brothers or her father. She locked the screen without replying, too, which would've confirmed it if I'd had any doubts. "Anyway. Eli, what do you say you come to my place on Friday? Kara and I leave work early."

I blinked. Why was everyone pulling one-eighties lately?

"What are you doing?"

Mónica pinned me with a look—tried to, anyway. People really didn't listen when I said those didn't work on me. "We're doing things my way, remember?"

Even if I didn't, it was becoming crystal clear she wasn't going to let me forget. Or live it down.

I pressed my mouth together. No way was I giving her the satisfaction of getting a response out of me.

I might not keep her from whatever it was that she was thinking, but that was all the leeway I was comfortable giving her.

18

ELI

You are better at taking care of people than you realize.

Patient, too, but I already knew you were. I just didn't realize you'd have to be patient with me. I'll get there, though.

It's... hard, for lack of a better word. I can't remember the last time I felt like this. My whole life, being on top of every problem, having a thousand contingency plans, it was the only way. I never felt... I've never felt like I could show weakness or uncertainty. Everyone always looked up to me for solutions, for leadership.

I like it, don't get me wrong. I am a leader. I always have been. My skin is already prickling just thinking about whatever Mónica is planning, and she's the person I trust the most.

I am not comfortable following someone else.

But I think, maybe in more recent months, I kind of forgot that being a leader doesn't mean handling everything on my own. I lost sight of that, and suddenly facing the fact that you were here, depending on me, opened my eyes to it.

It's not your fault. I think anything else would've done me in as well.

And now I guess I have to remember how to lead in a healthier way. It seems so easy on a theoretical level, doesn't it?

- Erika

I was brimming with excitement. I didn't usually do that. My emotions tended to be more contained, more introspective.

I'd been waiting for this for what felt like ages. It had been less than a week, but my brain didn't much care for objective facts like those.

> **KARA**
>
> Mónica wanted me to ask if everything's set up
>
> We're not doing much, so we can go and help if you need us to

> **ELI**
>
> i'm good
>
> everything's ready

> **KARA**
>
> You're really efficient

JUST ONE RULE

I didn't know what to say to that, so I just tucked my phone inside the locker room and snapped the metal door closed. I'd only come back to the locker room to change into the clothes Mónica had instructed. I was used to wearing my suit, but she'd requested a different outfit. Well, at first she'd asked if I'd be okay being naked. Nudity was part of the dress code, and I was comfortable with Sergio and the others who opted for it, but it wasn't my thing.

I understood the rubber suit could get in the way for some forms of play, though. That was why I kept other options in the locker—like what I was wearing now. The crotchless undies and binder left me more exposed than I usually liked, but it was okay.

Mistress had already agreed to meet me here at the club after She was done at the gym, too. It helped. She said Abel had forced Her to take a day off, but he couldn't stop Her from going as a client. I'd giggled a bit when She said it. It really was strange to see this grumpier side of Mistress Erika.

I went upstairs again. We were using the impact play room.

Most of the rooms had impact toys, either visible or inside one of the cabinets or wardrobes lined up against the walls, but the impact play room had more of the furniture—benches, sawhorses, St. Andrew's crosses bolted to the floor.

Mónica hadn't been too forthcoming about her plans—which meant they probably involved me suffering some—but I hadn't asked many questions, either. I'd just written down the way she wanted me to set up the room and what time I had to tell Mistress Erika to show up. Mónica was going to arrive before Her, so she'd be in charge of everything else. I just had to kneel and follow commands.

It was all I wanted, so there was no way I'd start complaining.

I was double—more like triple—checking that everything in the room was perfect when Kara stormed inside.

I frowned.

It wasn't like Kara couldn't bear the sight of a cross, or a paddle, but she still avoided this room most of the time.

"Okay?"

I cleared my throat. Shit. I must be more nervous than I'd first thought—or more affected by all the changes to my usual routine within these walls.

Kara barely faltered in her step. "Yeah. Of course! Mónica wanted me to help her with her boots and stuff, but I was feeling too jittery, so I said I'd come here and help you instead."

There was not a lot for her to help with, but I was still stuck on the fact that she was in this room.

"We can move to the Littles' room."

Kara frowned. "Are we switching plans? Mónica didn't say anything, and you're here…?"

"No switching plans." I shifted on my feet. I didn't know why I was struggling so much to get the message across. There was no reason to feel uncomfortable around Kara. She was always sweet to me. "But today's about impact play. Right?"

Kara's eyes widened then. They were pretty—a stormy shade of blue. She said once they were the same color as her grandma's.

"I don't actually know. I mean, you'd think so, but D-types love messing with our heads, so who knows." She shrugged. Her voice was doing that thing where it went softer and sounded more childlike. "But even then, I want to be here for Mistress Erika, and I don't mind watching Mónica spanking someone, and if it's something else, I'll just leave and come back later."

I didn't think whatever we were going to do was as simple as a spanking, but Kara had to know as much. And I'd been there when Mónica ran a workshop on bastinado. It was right before Kara and Mónica started dating, and Erika had taken Kara under her wing. She'd looked a bit... shocked, maybe, but she had been all right.

And Mónica wouldn't put her sub in danger, even if she wasn't as... careful—as she'd put it—as Mistress Erika was.

"Okay. Can you check the shelves with the dams?"

Sometimes the people in charge of restocking them—there was a rotating schedule between the Founders and some of us who volunteered—missed a few expired ones. I hadn't heard of anything happening because of it—most people still checked before ripping the packages open. But I liked going over them and clearing the expired ones.

Some people might not think to double-check, or they might have vision issues or anything else that meant they didn't see the expiration date.

"Okay!" Kara bounced happily to the cabinets to the side. I wondered if she was going to have all that energy when Mistress Erika arrived. It was disconcerting to have all that exuberance in this room. Some people—like Danny, and probably Carlos—liked impact play because of the adrenaline that came with it. The appeal of it for me had to do with the... ritual of it. The patterns. The cadence. Someone bouncing around clashed with that mental picture. "How's Erika been, anyway? I text with her, but I can never read her moods."

I didn't know what to say to that either. Mistress was very forward in Her texts. I didn't think I'd ever struggled with the meaning of them, but I didn't know how She was doing, either. It bothered me. They were expectations I'd set on myself. I was aware. I couldn't control that initial reaction, though. Maybe I'd be able to one day, but that day was not today.

"I think She's feeling better."

It was the least adequate way to respond to Kara's question. A part of me wished I had brought my notebook with me. Phones weren't allowed upstairs, but if I was having a harder time on a particular day, I'd bring a notebook. I didn't use it often, and it was more awkward than using my phone, but it helped.

I wouldn't want to use my phone when I was up here, anyway. Here was about slipping into a service mindset, where I was just a sub and there was no anxiety about trying to navigate the world around me.

"That's good," Kara said.

Right. I'd been telling her about Mistress.

She *was* feeling better. At least, I thought She was. It was hard to assess. I didn't want to be hovering, to be checking in constantly. If I were in Her shoes, that would only amp up my anxiety and make things worse.

So I'd mostly been sticking to our new routines. I cooked and added ingredients to the app Mistress had shared with me for grocery shopping. I wrote in my journal and memorized all the messages Mistress left in Hers for me. I hadn't gone out with anyone since Mónica and Kara hosted me on Friday, but I didn't think that meant I was lagging behind.

I was talking with people, and agreeing to meet up with them didn't mean I had to do it every day. No way could I gather the energy to do that. The mere thought gave me the shivers.

And at night, I was an object for Mistress. Another shiver ran through my body, but this one was the good kind.

Mónica walked inside the room before I could get lost in the memories. It happened more often than I would've thought when I agreed to this. There was just something...

Last night, Mistress Erika told me I was to kneel in front of Her and keep Her clit wrapped between my lips. If She wanted to get off, She'd use me, but I was to stay there. Clit-warming? I knew of cockwarming, but I wasn't sure the equivalent was as… well-known.

People were missing out.

By the end of it, I felt literally drunk on Mistress. She had to drag me upward and take me to the bathroom and basically put me in the shower Herself. There had been a hint of shame there, of the humiliation that I couldn't snap out of it and do something so basic.

I'd come so hard when Mistress touched me after She deemed me clean enough.

"Ready to start, you two?" Mónica asked.

Kara yelped while I nodded. "Yes, Ma'am."

"Why us two? I've done nothing!" Kara's voice went higher than I thought it could go. "This time."

"Baby girl." There was a warning in Mónica's voice, but it wasn't like when Mistress warned me. Hers was softer. There was so much adoration in two simple words. "Do we need to revisit the idea of speech restriction?"

Kara swallowed. "No, Ma'am."

Mónica lasted all of two seconds before she beckoned Kara closer and squeezed her tight.

"Sit down by one of the benches. Everyone knows you're off limits tonight."

I swore there was some huffing before Kara leaned on her tiptoes to kiss Mónica and did as her Domme asked.

Mónica just shook her head in fond exasperation. Then her attention shifted back to me.

"Your Mistress is at the club, but I wanted to go through what I've planned before she comes up here. Is that okay with you?"

I inhaled sharply. "Yes, Ma'am."

"Today is a test for you."

Huh?

I frowned. My breath caught in the back of my throat. Wasn't today meant to be about Mistress Erika?

My confusion had to be clear on my face, even when most of it was covered, because Mónica laughed. "And a reward, I suppose. Are you okay with wearing a blindfold?"

Another swallow. "Yes, Ma'am."

My heart sped up. Wearing a blindfold was not something that gave me pause. I'd been here while wearing a blindfold—and headphones—plenty of times.

My nerves came from trying to keep up.

Mónica had a knack for mind games not everyone knew about if they hadn't known her for long. She wasn't just a Leather Domme with a soft spot for Littles. There were more layers to the way she dominated.

"And headphones?"

Funny I'd just been thinking about those. "Yes, Ma'am."

There was less hesitation this time—I dealt better with direct questions that weren't preceded by statements meant to destabilize. Even if I liked the jumbling of thoughts.

"Good." Mónica moved to the one wardrobe she'd asked me not to touch. I wasn't surprised when she pulled out the two items she'd just asked me about. The blindfold was the kind made with thick padded leather. It was higher quality and completely covered my sight without being uncomfortable. The headphones were high quality, too. I'd worn both items before. "I want you on your hands and knees once you put these on. After that, people we've vetted are going to walk in here, and they're going to use you. The ways you'll be used have been cleared with your Mistress."

I gasped. Mistress and I had talked about free use while in the club, about fantasies that resembled glory holes and the kind of objectification that turned me into a sex doll for everyone to have their way.

Getting the words out was hard, but I didn't think it had to do with my usual struggles. "What's the test, Ma'am?"

Mónica didn't answer right away. She just watched me for a second. I noticed she was wearing more proper gear—a full leather ensemble. She didn't usually bother with all the fanfare—which I thought was only out of spite to annoy Mistress—but it meant she was covering all her bases today.

She grinned. I couldn't tell what she'd been searching for, but whatever she found must've satisfied her. "You just have to tell which one is your Mistress after everyone's done. You get bonus points for every other person you get right."

I put a hand to my chest. It felt like a silly gesture, but it was the only thing I could think of doing. Obviously, hearts didn't just pop out of people's bodies, but I couldn't say I was too eager to test that theory.

"How do I...?" I cleared my throat. Too many questions were bubbling up to the surface. I was never too good at prioritizing them.

Mónica lifted her hand before I could make more of a jumbled mess of my thoughts. The command in her posture was all I needed to breathe out and gave me permission to sink to my knees. It was easier to think when I had to look up to meet her gaze.

"Each person will use a different toy or play with a different body part. You don't have to keep track of the order or anything like that." Mónica smiled as if she was doing me a favor. I wasn't sure that she was, but I wasn't the impulsive type who would blurt that out. "Oh, and the more points you get, the more orgasms in your near future, so... I'd pay attention."

How was I supposed to pay attention? Well, I *could* pay attention. I was good at that. I just wasn't sure what paying attention here would look like. Without sight or hearing, I was… fifty percent confident I could tell Mistress's touch from everyone else's. Maybe sixty-five percent.

I wasn't sure about the rest.

Whenever I'd played with sensory deprivation at the club, figuring out whose touch belonged to whom had never been a priority. It was never a part of the scene, and I couldn't say it was something I stressed about or even focused on.

I wanted to do it today.

I wanted to do good.

Mónica handed me the blindfold and headphones. I grabbed the blindfold first, strapping it easily around my eyes. There was a tiny glitch, a second of panic right before darkness wrapped around me. My thighs clenched at around the same time. Fear and lust often went hand in hand for me —the controlled kind of fear, at least.

I was expecting to feel the headphones in my outstretched hands next. Instead, there was some shuffling before a familiar thud against the wooden floors. Warmth made me stand on alert.

"This is about Erika, too, don't worry." That was where the warmth came from; Mónica on her knee, leaning close to whisper in my ear. Even knowing now, a shiver racked down my spine. "We have to show her you're really bonded with her, don't we?"

I whimpered. I couldn't help it. I just wanted touch, for the scene to begin. It might be my first time with something like this, but I was craving it. I wanted to be surrounded, to drown in sex and anything else the Domms Mónica had invited wanted to give me.

"Ready?" Mónica asked.

Sometimes I wondered if the Domms at the club could read my mind. The ones who had been around long enough certainly acted as if it was a given.

"Yes, Ma'am."

The foam of the headphones muffled my already covered ears. Nothingness surrounded me for a second. I could only listen to my rapid heartbeat.

A nudge to my calf made me jolt.

I frowned.

Then it made sense. I wasn't supposed to kneel.

Getting into a position without any frame of reference felt strange. Destabilizing. I wouldn't be surprised if I was trembling or clumsier than I usually was.

I had to be in the right position, though. Muscle memory was surely a thing, regardless of other senses.

There were no more nudges, so I took it as a yes. It meant that I could breathe out, that I could relax into the position, focus on my breathing enough that I could think.

I didn't know if people were already swarming the room, or how many of them there were. I didn't know what tricks they had up their sleeves—because there was no way there wouldn't be any trickery. Which all meant I had to be at the top of my game.

I had to make Mistress proud. Mónica, too. She was trusting me to do this, using me to pull Mistress out of Her funk.

The certainty clung to my skin as a second armor and a gust of fresh air.

I wiggled on my spot, less than an inch, just what I needed to feel more stable.

I was going to do this, no matter what.

Lubed fingers pressed against my rim. I didn't know how much time had passed, but the touch made me tense up before leaning into it. I gasped.

I knew I should be trying to guess whose fingers, but it was already a challenge. I had to fight the urge to sink further, to let go and just feel.

I had no idea who it could be.

Not Mistress. She didn't prep me like this, starting with two fingers circling the wrinkled skin. Probably not Abel, either. I'd never done anal with him, but he looked like the person who would go one finger at a time. Sergio talked about it a lot. He'd probably give a rimjob first, too.

The fingers didn't press in. They just stayed there.

Not León, then? I doubted he ever played the long game, but I didn't see him play much outside of workshops on impact play.

I squirmed.

The fingers disappeared. I didn't have time to wonder if I'd done something wrong before they were on me, again.

Maybe León then.

Danny talked often about how he used the element of surprise.

The hit of the fingers against skin didn't make me yelp, but it was close. I covered it with a half grunt. I didn't know how convincing it was. Without the headphones, I was sure at least one of them would be leering, mocking me for the sound. I could picture them easily.

I didn't even know who I was supposed to picture exactly, but it didn't feel too important. In my head, it was everyone in our inner circle. I'd make sense of the logistics later.

Even if it wasn't all of them, they had to be from the inner circle. Mónica and Mistress wanted me to guess their identities. Even if Mistress was more demanding than Mónica, She wasn't cruel.

Well—I licked my lips. She could be cruel, but not the kind of cruel Domm that set their sub up for failure without letting them know.

If She thought I could do this, the Domms about to use every inch of my body had to be Domms I was familiar with.

Maybe subs, too?

JUST ONE RULE

I furrowed my brows. Mónica had never mentioned a role. She'd said people.

I hung my head as the fingers hit my hole squarely once more. With more people joining our group, there were too many to keep track of.

Mónica? She wasn't the biggest on impact play, but...

Yeah. It could be Mónica. She had calloused hands, too, and she'd been here first. It would make sense that she started out while everyone else got ready.

Shit. I'd known it would be hard, but not *this* hard.

Moans slipped past my lips as Mónica alternated between hitting and massaging my rim. I didn't know if she was scared of doing something else or if this was her way of prepping me for what was to come. I was still going with the theory that it was Mónica behind the touch.

And I was still certain that this was going to be an even more demanding scene than I'd first thought.

Eventually, the hitting, tapping, or whatever it was—I couldn't always identify what was being done to me without looking—stopped, and Mónica's fingers slid fully into me. I clenched around the digits right away. I groaned as she stretched me open.

Then I groaned again when she left me gaping around nothing.

I held my breath, too, waiting for the next person, the next thing to hit me.

Shit.

I might not be the best at telling what was going on without looking, but I could tell when someone caressed my back with a single tail whip.

Hard to get that one mixed up with any other toy.

I moaned. Nothing had happened yet, but my entire body responded as if it had happened. It had to be Mistress or León. They were the only ones who wielded a single tail. Did

Tony, too? But Mónica was here, so I doubted Tony would've been invited. Mistress still had him on a trial basis of sorts, too.

I breathed out.

It didn't matter. Well, it mattered, but I could figure it out after the first hit came. That was when the building anticipation left me, and I could think through the release.

The twisted leather hit my upper back. I screamed. It was part shock, part need to let out everything that had been building up, and part the pain that came from it. My elbows buckled. I needed a second to put myself back together.

The next hit came right before I could do it.

I gasped, air leaving my lungs.

Both León and Mistress would've pulled that. The two of them loved giving subs a challenge. I frowned.

There had to be something I could do, some way to tell them apart. They'd learned from each other, though. They attended each other's workshops all the time and talked about all the best floggers. If there was anyone who could play tricks on a sub to get them mixed up, it was the two of them.

After ten hits, ten times I screamed and fought to stay in perfect position, I wasn't any closer to figuring it out.

No more hits came.

I sobbed. The tears just came out. A hand wrapped around my wrist until I lifted my hand. I didn't realize how hard I was digging the heels of my palms against the floor until I had to lift it. Pins and needles ran through it. I winced as the person intertwined our fingers together. Then there was a squeeze.

Oh.

I squeezed back.

And that gave me my answer.

"Green, Sir."

JUST ONE RULE

It wasn't Mistress's hands, and everyone knew my nonverbal safe words.

There was a pause, and León let go of my hand. I bet Mistress was scowling at him for giving himself up.

It was a funny thought—not that I had a lot of time to relish in it. A bulbous dildo slid into me what felt like only seconds later.

A rubber-clad body draped on top of me.

One of the pups.

I wiggled, pushing to ease the toy in.

It was Cece.

The two pups were just as energetic and vigorous with their fucking, but Cece was slightly more patient when it came to letting whoever they were fucking adjust to the girth of their monster cocks.

Mitt-clad hands pressed against mine. Cece's head rested on my shoulder, burrowing against my neck. I panted.

I supposed it was a respite, easier to bear than a single tail. On its own, it would be, even when Cece's pace had me trembling, the force in their thrusts making me keen as I cried out for… something, anything else that would grant me release.

My brain kept whirling with possibilities, too. Whenever I wasn't drowning in what was happening right here and now, I was trying to step ahead, trying to figure out who was left, what they'd do—when I was going to be used by Mistress.

Keeping track of time was strange. Having no sort of feedback added up to that sense of… Disconnect wasn't the right word. I was very much connected to my body, but I was also floating in some kind of ether, neither here nor there, with little to anchor me.

I was sweating, Cece helping every time I slipped and tried to buckle down to my elbows. Pressure, heat, everything kept building up. Even without the blindfold, I wasn't sure I'd be able to see straight—to focus my eyes on anything.

The sounds escaping my lips were muffled. Hearing oneself always felt weird with headphones on. I was sure I was being louder than usual. If anyone asked, I'd pull off my best impression of a brat and blame Cece. They kept pounding me, and there was nothing on my clit, nothing pushing me to the orgasm I'd been chasing since I got on my knees.

Then again... I blinked behind the blindfold. I wasn't supposed to come until Mistress said so, was I?

It was a rule.

Shit.

I started trembling more visibly.

Cece let go of me. It took everything not to scream at them, not to protest the absence, the emptiness. León must've set a new habit because Cece nudged my hand.

I panted, my chest heaving up and down.

"G-green."

My voice warbled. I couldn't hear it right, but I knew it did.

I needed air. I needed—

A finger slipped between my lips, pressing against my tongue. I swallowed back the gag reflex I hadn't struggled with in a while.

The pressure increased.

Mistress. It wasn't just the fact that I'd had Her fingers deep down my throat plenty of times or the saltiness of Her skin. There was an assertiveness to the way She handled me —the way She took what She wanted without question.

My entire body sagged. She didn't let me bathe in that relief.

No, She pushed me until I was on my knees, hovering by Her hold on my mouth and jaw. I whimpered.

I didn't know how to picture Her. Was She disappointed? I didn't know if I was behaving as She expected or not. Was She playfully mocking me? Thinking of all the ways She could be degrading me if I didn't have the headphones on?

I counted my heartbeats, held my breath. I still didn't know what to focus on. Mistress, obviously. I just didn't know how, other than by letting Her move me around.

19
―
ELI

"Mistress."

I was pretty sure I'd butchered the word. Her fingers were still in my mouth, and She wasn't letting go. My thighs trembled as She lifted me higher, kept me unsteady, knees off the floor. I'd had to tell Her, though, to let Her know I knew.

I'd always know.

I couldn't foresee a time when I wouldn't know, when my body wouldn't respond to Mistress Erika differently than it did everyone else.

There was a pause after I uttered the honorific. I might be imagining it, but the air around us felt heavy, charged with unspoken truths.

I didn't know if that made sense or not. I didn't care if it didn't, but I wondered what She'd say when we talked about this. Her perspective tended to align with mine, but it also brought up details I hadn't thought of. There was a depth to the way She processed interactions and power dynamics. A part of me was jealous of it and wanted to soak up as much of it as I could.

She took off the headphones.

My ears popped.

There wasn't any heavy music playing—or any music at all—or people talking. I still needed a second to adjust to the shift in pressure. In stimuli I could find.

"You're so good to me." Erika's voice trembled. She let go of my jaw and pulled me all the way up. After a while, it was easy to think of me as a puppet, strung around by whoever was closest to me. There was a sense of safety in the metaphor. "Wrap your arms around my neck."

I gasped. I was still recovering, my back burning.

I did what She said regardless—but I had questions. "Yes, Mistress."

She wouldn't whip me again, but I didn't know what to expect. Gaining my hearing back didn't help matters if no one was speaking or making any kind of noise I could identify.

I still didn't even know how many people were watching, surrounding us.

Mistress Erika was wearing a new latex suit. She'd shown it to me when She got the delivery. It was black and skintight. It looked like a plain suit at first, covering her body from the neck down, but it came with a matching garter belt. I could only imagine the kind of things She'd store in there.

But anyway, I knew it was the new suit because the latex always felt different when it wasn't as used, and Her other suits didn't have the same cut around Her neck. Mistress had shown me Her entire collection once.

She hadn't tried the suit on in front of me, though, so I was now itching for the moment She took the blindfold off.

I had a feeling it would still be a while.

"Can you tell me who was who so far?"

I hid against the crook of Her neck first. I almost headbutted Her in the process, but I didn't have enough working brain cells to feel too self-conscious about it.

"Mónica. León. Cece. You."

"Impressive." Her lips ghosted over my temple. I shivered. "Do you want to keep going after I have my way with you?"

I gulped. Was there more? "As you wish, Mistress."

It wasn't lack of consent or lack of enthusiasm. The enthusiasm was in the fact that She'd choose. Mistress would keep the fantasy up—the dream that She was the one who made all decisions about my body.

"That's right." There was a hint of pleasure in Her voice that hadn't been there before. She sounded firmer, too, like… Like she used to, before I showed up and unintentionally upended Her life. "You can be loud, but letting go of my neck or kicking anyone means the scene ends."

I nodded at the same time as I spoke. "Yes, Mistress."

I could keep my feet planted on the floor. I might—clearly—not be the best yet at staying quiet, but I was good at staying still. Mistress Erika was aware of that distinction, too. I kept forgetting to bring up how I struggled more to keep things within ever since I'd moved in, but She knew.

It wasn't wishful thinking. It was in the way She acted around me, the secret smiles She shared, and the way She studied me. There weren't many things She missed when it came to the subs She played with.

A slight buzz had me clenching my thighs.

I recognized it.

Not that long ago, we'd been in Her office, and I'd had to be the one who used it. Mistress *had* said She wanted to train me on it.

Now the warning about kicking someone made more sense. Electroplay made staying still even more of a challenge.

I could do it, though, I—

The yelp that slipped from my lips was not one I'd ever admit to outside these walls. Mistress had just placed the wand against my inner thigh, on that soft skin where my hip and leg met.

My chest heaved. It took a second to take stock of my body. It felt like the thing to do. The spot where she'd zinged me burned, buzzing from the unfamiliar sensation.

I hadn't moved, though.

I wasn't any less wet, either. When I squirmed as that thought materialized in my head, it was for completely different reasons than the threat of another zing.

Mistress didn't use a high setting when She used the wands. She said it heightened the risk for complications too much when a lower setting could grant as much of a reward.

I saw what She meant, even though nothing about this felt like a low setting.

It all felt high stakes, high risk—even if the risk wasn't related to the electricity zapping through my skin.

The next zap came on my other thigh, around the same spot. I moaned. My fingers clenched around my elbows. There was no way I'd risk letting go of Her neck.

I realized I was buckling my knees inward before the next zap came. I knew Mistress enough to know where it was going to hit, blindfold or not.

If I hadn't realized, the low kick would've done it. I jolted, standing upright before I could process it had been Mistress correcting my posture.

I tried to babble something—some excuse, some protest, some apology. I didn't know. Sounds might not be muffled anymore, but I wasn't sure any of it had been understandable. It didn't feel like it had.

"Mistress."

It was the only word that made sense to use as a plea.

As gratitude?

I didn't know.

There were too many emotions running through my body, too close to the surface and yet too muddled by the needs of my body to properly tell them apart. Dissecting would come later. Now, my throat dried, and my heartbeat sped up as I tried to guess when Mistress would hit next.

Not where—that one was obvious.

But when.

My knees buckled again when it finally happened. I was close to losing my grip on Her. The first zap was always the worst, the one that left no time to prepare for what was coming.

Blindfolded, it turned out that applied to all of the zaps that came from the wand.

Mistress moved Her hand to the back of my neck. "You're getting what you wanted, aren't you?"

The words were spoken against my ear. I shivered.

Another zap.

Another yelp.

Another second when my grip on reality almost slipped, when I had to tighten my grip around Her neck, and I fought every instinct in my body that wanted to run away from the overstimulation it was being put through.

I didn't know if I was feeling too much or too little, if I was floating too high or not high enough. Mistress's words kept me there, in that space in the middle of everything and nothing. I was aware of my body trembling, of the sobs that started as I hid my face against her neck. But the overstimulation of my body was nothing compared to what happened in my head, all the emotion and freedom and whirls through paths I didn't have access to any other way.

"Mistress," I gasped.

There were no other words, no other dialogue possibilities.

Not enough air, either.

My legs trembled too much. I felt too high in whatever hormones ran havoc through my body to do anything, to *want* to do anything. I just wanted to exist for Her, to be used by Her.

"We should've talked about recording this," She said. Her grip on the back of my neck tightened. I gasped, heart slamming against my rib cage. "You could see what a slut you are, not even trying to move away while everyone is doing whatever they want to your body."

"Mistress."

Please.

Stop.

More.

Keep talking.

Have mercy.

"Shh." Mistress pressed her lips against the top of my head. But it had me keening, crying. The zaps kept going. I couldn't keep track any longer. There were just currents to pointlessly avoid, and heat, and pressure, and Mistress's words, and my body struggling with the thing to focus on. "You're just going to keep taking whatever we want to give you, aren't you?"

Whimpering was the only sensical sound that came out of my lips. I was sure I was trying to say something, but I couldn't put too much effort into figuring out what it was. I couldn't worry about it, either. Rather, there was no room for worrying, for concern, or... anything that wasn't the way my body was being pushed to the limit.

The way my *mind* was being pushed the same way.

Something clattered on the floor.

I gasped.

A part of me kept waiting for the next zap. It took another second to process the sound—the wand gone.

I trembled, my weight shifting toward Mistress.

"There's one more person, slut," Mistress said. I tried to catch some air. "Guess who it is, and one of those orgasms you've earned comes from me."

Shit.

I couldn't get my legs to stand straight.

For once, it didn't seem to matter. Mistress carried my weight easily. I thought I'd be pushed onto my hands and knees again. Instead, I was on top of latex—of Mistress. My back was to Her chest, and She held my thighs open.

Time still felt funny around me, not working quite right. It meant that I couldn't tell how long it was, but then I felt the familiar sensation of a dam covering my groin.

Seconds later (probably), a tongue was there, flicking against the skin.

I didn't know what it was about it, but as that tongue flickered in and out, teasing, I started spasming like I hadn't before. It was the softest of touches, but my body didn't seem to care.

Sobs erupted out of my throat. It was as raw as I'd ever felt. Heat crept up to my face, my cheeks. I writhed in Mistress's hold.

"Keep going."

Oh?

Right. The tongue had stopped.

I whimpered.

"Who is it, slut?" Mistress grabbed me by the chin. I didn't resist. I wouldn't know how to start doing it. "You know everyone here, don't you? Tell me, and the blindfold is off."

I hadn't even considered that I might want it off. Now that the offer was there, though, my skin was suddenly itching. I was suddenly aware of the sweat pulling around the worn leather.

"Kara," I croaked out.

Kara was volunteered for oral every time. She was good, but she always started small. Shy, almost.

The blindfold came off.

I gasped, reaching for air I didn't think I'd had until now. I knew it was illogical. My air flow had never been cut off, but my body didn't care for logic. It cared to fill my lungs, to cry out louder while I blinked my eyes open and tried to bring the room into focus.

Mistress grabbed me. She always did when I found myself too overwhelmed. She forced me to look down, to locks of blonde hair kneeling between our legs. Kara looked up at me through hooded eyes. There was a level of mischief there.

"How did you know?" Her voice was raspier than usual, but I didn't think she'd been eating me out long enough. Maybe Mónica had been using her before this? "I've never done you before."

I grunted. Her lips wrapped around my clit before I could even think of an answer.

Mistress pushed two fingers into my mouth before I could do it. "Objects don't talk unless their Mistress addresses them, little one. You can ask later."

For a second, Kara pretended to frown. It was easy to see when it was pretend—a playful scowl.

And now that she was more confident, all her energy quickly shifted to pressing her tongue against my clit, lapping at it through the dam as if she was dying to drown in my fluids.

"Mistress."

I turned my face toward Her. I needed more, but I didn't know how to ask for it. I didn't know what that would look like, what more meant.

As it turned out, it didn't matter. The moment my head rested against Her shoulder, all bets were off.

I couldn't tell what came over me. But those sobs, those spasms that had felt almost foreign? They came back full force. I wasn't in control of my body. I was sobbing as hard as I ever had, trembling from head to toe. The tears mixed in with the sweat that clung to my skin. It made me sob harder. I didn't know why.

Mistress held me tight.

For the first time, I truly didn't know where to focus. Before, it had been Mistress. She was my anchor. Right now, I didn't know. Emotions had never been so close to the surface, pouring out of my body so freely. I couldn't bottle them down. There was no cap to be found, no tape to put over them in hopes to make them disappear.

My entire body hurt, but it also craved. My head…

My head was a fucking mess.

"I've got you, Eli." Mistress pressed Her lips to the top of my head.

I wondered if it was the thing that undid me. But suddenly my mind was replaying that moment in my—now old—room. My uncle's reddened face. The shock as I ran down the stairs with only my phone in hand.

"I want my things back," I garbled.

There was no way anything about my tears was attractive right now. Or about the way my fists grabbed Mistress's arms desperately enough the thought occurred to me that I might leave bruises. That should be something I worried about, right? I didn't want to do that. More flashbacks I hadn't even thought of in years pushed through the fog in my head. I flinched. The tremors were strong enough I didn't know if anyone could miss them. Kara was still there. Mónica sat next to us, her hand on Kara's nape guiding her. I couldn't really tell what she was doing. I couldn't muster the energy to ask why they were doing it. I didn't know why I would care.

I only knew that the pressure kept building up, the heat kept amping up, until all my muscles were drawing taut.

I screamed. It was high pitched, higher than I even knew I was capable of.

The new tremors running down my body were different. They were aftershocks of the weirdest orgasm I'd ever had.

I didn't care.

I just wanted—needed—Mistress.

"I want to get my things," I said again, enunciating more clearly. Mistress tightened Her hold on me. The new flashbacks flooded me again. I kept trembling. I was sure Kara had pulled back, but I didn't want to look. "And I want a hug from my mother."

My eyes widened.

I hadn't meant to say that, had I?

Another sob racked down my spine, another shiver before I broke down in more tears. Nothing but those tears seemed to exist. Kara whimpered. Mistress and Mónica cursed under their breaths. I was too busy figuring out why I'd blurted that out. I didn't blurt things out. It just wasn't how I worked. It made no sense.

I didn't even know if I—

I'd just thought back to one of the few good days back when I was still living under my parents' roof. When things hadn't been anywhere near perfect, but I'd been trying to make them work regardless.

And then—

Then there was a blanket draped around me. Arms tightened around me, too. Mistress's, Mónica's, Kara's. There was shuffling, some repositioning. More arms and weight covering me.

I shut my eyes and hid against Mistress. I didn't think I could watch without completely breaking apart.

"That's it." Mistress hummed. I frowned. "Let it all out. We've got you."

I shivered. I wanted to do as She said. I just didn't know if there would ever come a time when I'd let it all out. I didn't know what that would look like, either, what kind of hollow shell it would leave behind.

But I liked the warmth of everyone wrapping around me. I liked the way it spread across my chest, filling me in ways nothing ever had. I liked the whispered words of praise, even if I didn't have an answer for them.

None of them said it, but I felt it anyway. This was my family. I didn't care how mushy it sounded. They'd always be my family.

I didn't want a different one.

Not really.

"We've got you," Mistress repeated.

Arms tightened more—somehow. I didn't know who it was. It didn't matter.

I was safe here.

20

ERIKA

Fucking hell.

When Mónica had shared her idea for the evening, I hadn't expected that. Eli crying for its mother after an orgasm? I didn't think anyone could've prepared me for the way my heart shattered into a million pieces.

It wasn't something I could fix. It wasn't something I could replace, either.

"Mistress?"

I looked down at Eli. After driving us home, I'd wrapped it up in a blanket and moved us to the couch. I'd considered going to bed, but I thought Eli would need a moment to rehash what had transpired at Plumas before then. I liked the routine of talking in bed like we'd been doing, but I didn't like the idea of associating bedtime with open wounds and traumatic events.

"Yeah?"

Eli took a deep breath before it licked its lips. "Mónica said… today… had been about me."

"Yes?"

I frowned. Obviously, I knew what Mónica had been trying to say, but I'd bet anything that she didn't explain everything completely, so she'd left my sub with more questions than answers.

Or maybe she'd assumed I'd already talked to Eli about it while we'd showered after the scene—and after León had checked that he didn't go too hard on Eli's back.

It gulped. "What did she mean?"

I pulled Eli closer to me before I answered. I pressed my lips against the top of its head, too. Something I wanted to discuss, even more so after tonight, was that Eli needed more physical touch and affection than it had been willing to ask for. Maybe it hadn't even been aware.

The point was, Eli was going to get more of it if it was the last thing I did.

"I told you Mónica and I wanted to set something up for you back when you moved in, right?"

Eli nodded. I ran a finger across its cheekbone.

"Mónica has a theory that I basically... rushed too many steps ahead this time."

I licked my lips. I still didn't love her logic, but I supposed she'd had a point. Maybe talking about giving full access to a bank account the first day of someone going official was a bit too much. And maybe I'd let all those logistics swamp me and I'd completely forgotten about helping Eli through the fact that it had just lost their home and the trauma that came with it. My theory was that, subconsciously, I'd been very aware of that dismissal, and it was what had ultimately dragged me down.

"She said that you needed to prove yourself to me more than I needed to prove myself to you." It was paraphrasing it more than a bit, but Mónica's speech had included too many references to get my head out of my ass. "She also said that your trauma took priority to my hang-ups."

Eli frowned. I'd expected it, but I placed the pad of my thumb over its lips, shushing it. I understood Eli's instinct to jump in to defend me, but I didn't need nor deserve that defense. Acknowledging as much wasn't something that pulled me down. It didn't feel great, but it was true.

"She was right," I continued. Eli widened its eyes for a second, but it didn't fight. I pulled my thumb away from its mouth, resting against its jawline instead. "You *are* my responsibility. I *want* you to be my responsibility, and that means being held accountable for it."

Eli licked its lips. "Don't know what to say."

I figured as much. "I don't expect you to. I just needed the wake-up call, and I'm glad I got it."

More often than not, I had set goals and paths to take when I started a conversation. This time, I didn't. I truly didn't. Which meant I let the silence stretch around us, filling every space of the duplex that had only now started to feel like an actual home.

The beginnings of one, at least.

I should hit up my old therapist, because how come I had never taken the time to fill the space with the things that would bring me peace, warmth, and the sensations I associated with what a home needed to have?

Those were musings for another day.

"I'm embarrassed," Eli whispered.

I couldn't tell how long we'd been sitting in silence. It hadn't been uncomfortable, but now my attention centered on Eli once again.

Eli looked miserable—nowhere compared to how it had looked when it had cried for the family it had lost, but it was still close enough all the alarms were pinging inside my brain.

"What for?"

Eli shrugged while trying to hide a sniffle. "I don't... My mind just... strayed? I don't know."

"It makes sense." I hummed. "I have a feeling that you were repressing a lot."

Eli closed its eyes and worked on its breathing for a few seconds before giving an answer. It was a small thing, but there was something about a person taking a second to regulate themselves before engaging in any kind of discussion. It multiplied my respect for them tenfold.

"I wasn't hiding it from you," Eli said. It wasn't something I'd considered, but I had no interest in interrupting whatever Eli was working through. "Ash said... They said that the only red flag they saw in me was that I wasn't processing my trauma, and it was something that worried them."

"Is it going well with them?"

I never asked Eli about the therapy sessions. I was glad when it said it was comfortable with Ash, and I listened when it shared something, but anything else would feel too invasive. The journal method was there already. I didn't need —or want—anything else.

"Yeah." Eli's eyes lit up. "They're... hard on me sometimes, but they're understanding. I like that."

Not enough people had been understanding with Eli.

I didn't know when I'd finish picking up all the pieces that had shattered after Eli broke down in my lap, but it was clearly not today.

"Good."

"But, uh..." Eli squirmed. I pressed it harder against me. One of the first things I ever learned about Eli, and it was only amplified after it moved in with me, was that Eli didn't feel suffocated by weight or pressure. It caused the opposite effect. "I know what I said, but I don't... I don't want my mother. Maybe the idea of a mother, but not mine. And I..."

"Breathe."

Eli could use its phone, too. I'd made sure my sub was clutching it when I wrapped it in this makeshift blanket burrito I was sure the Littles in the community would disapprove of, but it worked for us.

"Yeah." Eli swallowed, a small smile grazing its lips before they looked up. "I don't think I ever mourned the loss, though. And it... piled up."

That was the understatement of the century.

"Biological family is complicated."

It seemed that I was turning it into a competition.

Eli hummed. "I was thinking... in Plumas... that you were my family. All of you. It made me happy."

My eyes misted over. I scrubbed a hand down my face.

This wasn't how today was supposed to go. It shouldn't be about me losing my grip completely. Mónica had been right. Tonight had to be about Eli.

I usually had better control on my emotions, dammit.

Breathe in, breathe out. I repeated the mantra a few times before I turned to look at Eli once more. It looked so small buried under the blanket. The weighted one Eli liked had been out of stock, and it wouldn't arrive until next month.

I pulled it up, blanket burrito included, until our foreheads connected.

There was a possibility that Eli wasn't the only one who needed more physical touch than it had first assumed.

It had never been a big thing before, but I couldn't deny the pull now. Not with Eli so close.

"I love you, Eli."

It was important that I said it out loud, that I used Eli's name and not one of the nicknames I used to either degrade or praise. It didn't matter that I wasn't usually one for verbal showings when I could use other ways to show that love.

Changes to how I expressed emotions were already underway.

"Love you." Eli's smile wobbled, its body swaying forward.

I met its lips before it could ask any questions.

"There's a lot more to talk about." Unsurprisingly, Eli made a face. Little did it know I'd been one hundred percent expecting it. "Use your phone."

"Uh?"

I sighed fondly. It wasn't a sound I was too used to. I liked it.

With my hands on Eli's waist—what would be its waist—I gave the bundle on top of me a squeeze. It was a good thing that we were still in the middle of winter, and I didn't run particularly hot. "You've been drained enough today. You don't have to push yourself."

It never had to.

It took a second for it to catch on to what I was saying, regardless. It proved my point better than anything else would have.

"Thank you, Mistress."

I gave Eli a look. Eli just unlocked the screen of their phone and opened the Notes app. I'd once asked why it didn't use texts. Eli had explained it hated what it looked like when opening a text thread with someone, and it was all messages coming from it with no responses in between.

I could understand that.

> *i feel very soft inside*
> *very tired*
> *but like my body is all jelly*

I snorted. "Yeah, makes sense."

Eli—and other subs—would sometimes cry after or during a scene. It was something we monitored closely. Eli had never cried as hard as it did today, though. There was no way I would've missed it, or that I wouldn't have heard of it the following day.

Eli pursed its lips.

> *i wanna talk about you too, Mistress*
> *Are you really feeling better? i feel responsible,*
> *even though i understand what you and*
> *Mónica said*

Truth be told, when I told Eli to use its phone, I'd still expected to lead the conversation. I didn't think it was going to barge in with questions and commentary the second it had the green light for it. It came as a slight surprise, but a welcome one.

"I am." I sighed. The words felt true as they slid from my tongue, my teeth, my lips. "I think I knew I wasn't giving you what you needed, and I needed to see that I could still do it. That was why tonight was important for me too."

Eli cocked its head to the side, then went back to typing.

> *For what it's worth, i've only wanted you... i*
> *only want you to be my Mistress. i never wanted to*
> *make things messy, or to make you doubt yourself*

I could feel the corners of my eyes softening as I took Eli in. "I know."

But i suppose i did need today. So thank you for giving it to me, Mistress

I shook my head. I usually waited for Eli to show me the screen, but it was easy to read at the angle it was holding the phone. "You don't have to thank me."

Eli scrunched up its face. It didn't scowl, but it got close. I pinched its side. It was pure instinct to do it. We didn't work without rules, without protocols and lines. I didn't want us to.

What did you want to talk about, Mistress?

"More rules," I said. Eli preened right away, its whole body straightening and leaning closer. The most honest smile grazed its lips, too. I traced it with a finger before I could keep talking, memorizing the way it shivered and parted its lips in response. "But more about your uncle, too."

Eli shook its head right away.

I frowned, but it was typing before I could ask.

i don't want to talk about him. i know it's not... the right thing, and i have to, but... there is nothing to talk about. He's not going to change his mind, and i'd still go no contact even if he did.

Eli all but shoved the phone in my face. I had to squint, the glare of the screen too bright. I got it when I read what it was saying, but I was not going to lie to myself and say the move hadn't annoyed me. It bordered on brat behavior more than I was comfortable with.

"I don't want to talk about your relationship with him, or

lack thereof." It was a topic I wished Eli discussed with its therapist, but not because I said so. "I want to talk about paying him a visit to get your things."

To Eli's benefit, it didn't shake its head right away this time. The result was the same, but it paused for two seconds before starting to type again.

> *You do what you want to do*
> *Seriously, i trust you, Mistress*
> *But I don't want any part of it*

I pursed my lips. It wasn't the answer I'd hoped for. But Eli did say it wanted its things back, and realistically speaking, I couldn't just find a duplicate of absolutely everything. Pieces of clothes and tech were easy enough, if they weren't out of stock already, but I couldn't replace mementos.

I wasn't a millionaire either—nowhere near close. Mónica and Tony were the ones with money. Ev, too, with a few more caveats. Mónica would agree to spending any amount on Eli if any of us asked, but that was beside the point.

"I'll take care of it, then." There were no protests or phones shoved in my face this time. I supposed it was as much as I could hope for, and Eli had to be exhausted. I reminded myself of that not so small fact. "As for rules…"

A high-pitched sound of excitement escaped it. Eli wiggled closer, too. It was ridiculous. I never understood the Domms who said all subs regressed the tiniest bit after a particularly hardcore scene up until this moment.

"Remember when we agreed you were to greet me on your knees when I walked inside?" I knew Eli hadn't forgotten, but I paused until it nodded anyway. "You are to come greet me, but not on your knees."

Eli was bobbing its head before the rule registered. Then it squinted its eyes.

It was… sweet.

Sweet was apparently an acquired taste, and I had no problem with it.

"We are going to hug." I breathed in and out. Ordering someone to hug me, even when it was for its benefit, was not something I had a lot of experience with. The words flowed from my mouth, but not as naturally as they would if, say, I was telling Eli to give itself an enema or stretch itself so that I could fist it. "Then you are to take care of my coat and shoes."

Eli's breath hitched. It nodded right away.

"Good."

I had more rules planned, but I didn't feel dread about imposing them in the same way I did before. Now I wanted to take it slow for the right reasons, to get Eli used to its new routines—as both a slave and my sex toy—without overwhelming it. It made such a stark difference, I knew I was going to berate myself for a while for not seeing it sooner.

It was a good thing I had the rest of the people at the club to set me straight.

There was no way I wouldn't have Mónica on my case for at least the next couple of months.

Speaking of which, I had promised I'd text her once I got Eli to get some sleep.

I hoped she realized that wouldn't happen right away.

"We should go to bed, slut." Eli only shifted its hips at the change in tone. "And you should eat me out before getting the rest you need."

Eli's eyes fluttered before the wrinkles around its eyes flattened. "Yes, Mistress."

"Clock's ticking."

It wasn't, but those eyes seemed to sparkle at the tease.

I didn't need to help Eli out of the blanket around its body. It just sprinted off the couch and all but carried me upstairs.

Maybe I shouldn't have teased.

Then again, seeing that energy, that excitement after the events of the evening?

All worth it.

21

ERIKA

MÓNICA

Moving company confirmed they'll be there at 16:00. Do you need backup?

ERIKA

Don't make it sound as if I'm going to war.

I should be fine, but I'll text if I can't make it.

MÓNICA

You'd better

I shook my head as I read Mónica's last text. She really was Mommy Domme material, regardless of the label she and Kara wanted to use. It was easy to see why all the age players in our community flocked to her. I was fine, though. The only reason I might need to text her was if I was still at the salon. I'd gotten an appointment as early as possible, but I'd also canceled all the classes I had today that none of the trainers at the gym could take over.

It was frustrating, but with the gym open all weekdays and mornings in the weekend, and most hair salons closing after Saturday noon, there really wasn't a good solution. At the beginning, I'd still tried to schedule everything for Saturdays. Not many people signed up for classes on the weekend, and they were usually quiet days a part-time trainer could handle without much fuss. Doing that, however, ate away from my time at the club, and my personal time in general.

It had been necessary when I was starting out, but not now. Sure, I had to look into hiring more people, but even then, I could afford canceling a couple of classes and not spending twenty-four hours inside the gym.

Did I always remember? No, but... Well, I had more motivation to right now.

> ELI
>
> are you busy?

> ERIKA
>
> What do you need?

I loved the self-care that came with getting my hair done, but I wasn't one to engage in lively conversation. I usually texted, handled things in the community app—which was thankfully now something of the past—or simply took some time to center myself. The hairdressers here understood that. It was why I didn't mind if they had longer waiting lists or if they took longer than they promised over the phone. It was worth it.

> ELI
>
> i'm just anxious about today
>
> i haven't changed my mind, i don't want to go and have to see him, but i don't want him to be shit to you either, and i don't know how to stop thinking about it

> **ERIKA**
> I can take care of myself, pet.
> Are you done with your chores?

> **ELI**
> i know
> and yes, Mistress
> meal prep is done, i journaled, and did the homework Ash sent me for the week

> **ERIKA**
> Good

I left the chat to send someone else a quick text. I hadn't wanted to leave Eli alone today, especially because I wouldn't have time to stop by my—our—place before meeting the movers and, consequently, Eli's uncle. I'd discussed it with Eli, but it had said it didn't want its routine moved, that it would feel worse.

I'd understood it, and I'd respected that Eli wanted to process on its own. That didn't mean I hadn't run through a list of contingency plans in my head.

> **ERIKA**
> You weren't working today, were you?

> **LEÓN**
> Do I wanna ask how you know my schedules?

> **ERIKA**
> You only work on Monday if someone's booked a genital piercing, and you're loud about those to get Danny off.

> **LEÓN**
> Fair
> What's up?

> **ERIKA**
> Are you busy?

> **LEÓN**
> I was planning on a hike with Dan later. Carlos has a thing with his sister, and Dan's moping
>
> Why?

> **ERIKA**
> Take Eli.

> **LEÓN**
> Is that an order?

> **ERIKA**
> You wish.

It wasn't the best, but it would actually work because it wasn't. I knew Eli wasn't the most active person out there. It wasn't something I cared about, but it meant that Eli's focus would have to be on the terrain and keeping up with the other two. If Danny was *moping* as León said, it was even better.

> **ERIKA**
> Text León.

> **ELI**
> …
>
> yes, Mistress

> **ERIKA**
> I'll text as soon as it's all done.

Eli might not have reception depending on the trail León took it on, but there was no benefit to pointing that out.

> **LEÓN**
>
> You know I don't mind, but why does it feel like I'm on babysitting duty?
>
> **ERIKA**
>
> You and Sergio are the only ones available.
>
> Sergio isn't what Eli needs right now.
>
> **LEÓN**
>
> And why are we texting?
>
> **ERIKA**
>
> Hair salon. Sorry.

I snorted. I knew León could sext like nobody's business, but he had an old man streak too when it came to complaining about texting. Nine out of ten times, even if he was supposedly part of the generation that hated cold calls—and all kinds of calls, really—he'd just call me point-blank.

I preferred giving people a warning before I called, but I actually didn't mind getting calls from León. I didn't think one was better than the other—there was ableism rooted in that discourse—but it felt refreshing. Or maybe being in my mid-thirties made me nostalgic for those parts of my childhood, but Abel was my age and he just looked at me funny when I talked about it.

It was weird that we were the oldest in the group, not that age came up a lot. Those of us in our thirties had close to a decade of both experience and work on the ground. The others were thankfully happy to listen, and learn, and deconstruct themselves. It was part of my vetting process. I preferred a club with more strict entry rules and less members than one flooded with microaggressions and a complete lack of accountability.

NOT TO SOUND TOO DRAMATIC, but the house looked… bleak. I was parked in front of it, waiting for the movers to arrive. They'd stay back—and there was a distinct possibility that I'd have to pay them for a job not done if the uncle had thrown out everything—but I still waited. I didn't want to confront the man until they were here. Doing that would only lead to an uncomfortable standby until anything could get done.

I was all for efficiency. Having to deal with him already felt like a waste of my time. I wasn't going to make it more unpleasant.

Thankfully, the movers weren't running more than five minutes late. They were friends with one of Mónica's brothers or something, so they had some idea of what was going on, too. I wasn't a fan of airing people's business, but it saved me some questions in this particular case.

I just nodded in their direction before approaching the detached house. It was closer to Mónica's than I'd first realized, but the style was different. Mónica's was inviting even from the outside. This one just looked like no one had touched it ever since they bought it.

Kind of similar to my duplex, actually, save for my bedroom.

I definitely had work to do there, but this wasn't the time to start organizing it.

After taking a deep breath and cracking my neck, I knocked on the door. Twice, for good measure. I truly didn't know what to expect. Eli had said it wouldn't feel comfortable introducing him to anyone, but there were a million ways I could interpret that.

About three minutes later, the door opened. It didn't creak; I'd give him that. A man's features immediately turned into a scowl as he gave me a once-over. I mimicked the posture. Men were nothing if not predictable.

"You have a package or something?"

"I'm Eli's girlfriend." I was not going to comment on that assumption. I just stood taller. "Are their things still in their room?"

Eli's uncle fell under the category that only interacted with Eli the Person, but using they/them still left a strange taste in my mouth. I wasn't misgendering it, but I wasn't… acknowledging everything that Eli was—everything it meant.

The man had the decency to look taken aback. A mixture of emotions flashed across his face.

Shock. Anger. Shame. Disgust?

I didn't have the time, or the inclination, to decipher them.

"Well?"

He didn't look like I'd expected. He was somewhere in his late fifties or early sixties, probably. Shaggy grey hair framed a face that hadn't seen a razor in at least a couple of weeks. Too many wrinkles turned his face into a perpetual downturned frown.

"It's all upstairs."

"Great." I'd made many plans, but none of them would've been good enough if he'd thrown out everything in a fit of rage. "I hired a moving company. We'll take care of it."

It wasn't open for discussion, and in his defense, he caught on to the fact right away.

"Second door to the left upstairs."

"Thanks."

The smile I gave him was strained at best. He didn't bother to return it.

Packing everything was easy. Fast. Eli wasn't a hoarder,

but I knew at least half of the things here had some sentimental value. Eli deserved to have them and be the one to decide what to do with them.

There was an album in one of the drawers in its nightstand. I traced the cover with one finger. It was bright blue, with a stock image of a group of people smiling in the middle of it. It felt heavy, too, but Eli hadn't said anything about an album.

Nevertheless.

It went in one of the cardboard boxes, surrounded by thick hoodies and fluffy blankets so it wouldn't get damaged. I'd ask about it once I was back home. It wouldn't be until much later because past me decided to cram everything into today, but I'd deal with it. Not like I had much choice.

"Is this all?" I asked the man.

I didn't know if Eli stored anything in the living room, or the kitchen, or anywhere else. And I might not feel favorable toward its uncle, but I wasn't going to ransack the entire place on a wild goose chase. It was a headache I didn't need.

Eli had said everything would be in its room, but it didn't hurt to ask.

"Yeah. Eli's very particular about personal space."

I snorted. Eli was many things, but that wasn't one of them. The evidence was clear as day in my duplex. Eli might've only lived there for a little over a month now, but its —admittedly few—things were already spread all over the place. A weighted blanket lived in the corner of my couch. The set of kitchen knives Eli swore by were displayed as a trophy on the kitchen counter—I wasn't even sure that they'd been used yet. Its things were mixed in with mine in the bathroom.

Sharing spaces or making a space its own was not something I'd seen it struggle with.

Even in the club, before Eli moved in with me, it wasn't

JUST ONE RULE

afraid to ask for what it wanted or needed in a room or for taking space in it.

I supposed it spoke more than anything I could've said or done about the... state of their relationship and how comfortable Eli felt around him. I wouldn't be surprised if keeping everything in its room had been its subconscious way of protecting itself from the conditional type of attachment they seemed to have.

"Well, then. I'm not going to wish you a good day, but I appreciate you not making this any harder than it could've been."

The man—yes, I was aware I didn't have his name, but I wasn't keen to rectify that—looked so out of place. It was funny in how pathetic it was, but I didn't stay to twist the knife.

He wasn't worth any more of my time—or Eli's for that matter.

ERIKA

> Movers are on their way to the duplex. I told Abel to move all the boxes to your room. We'll work through them one at a time.

ELI

thank you, Mistress

ERIKA

> How's the hike going?

Eli sent a picture instead of texting. I opened it to reveal a gingham blanket and a makeshift picnic in the center of it.

ELI

León says I have to tell you that you need to get me hiking boots

> ERIKA
> Of course he says that.

I wasn't even sure *I* had proper hiking boots. I probably did from when I was getting my certifications to work at a gym. I remembered one of the classes involved hiking because some gyms were setting up hiking groups and routes for a while there when it was trendy. I didn't think I'd used them since then.

> ELI
> he also says he can drive me back if you need me there, Mistress

> ERIKA
> You're sweet.
> Let me know when you head back home.

> ELI
> yes, Mistress

I dropped my phone into the passenger seat before I started the engine. I didn't know that I was any readier than I had been back when I asked María to come meet me before everyone else made it to the club, but it was time.

We had agreed to meet in a neutral space, so after double-checking with Abel that the spare key to the apartment I'd given him worked, and that he was there to meet the movers, I headed toward the beach.

I didn't care what Abel and Sergio said about their beach walks, it was way too cold, and there was too much white sand to make the experience pleasing.

María said it was quiet and not many people actually stopped there.

No one could say I wasn't trying.

At least the drive didn't take too long, and I could park

right around the area María had mentioned—by the lifeguard tower that had a giant graffiti of the Republican flag no one bothered to clean. How some people still defended the existence of a monarchy was beyond me.

Anyway.

The wind whipped my face as I got out of the car. I wasn't looking forward to the trek down the flimsy and poorly illuminated wooden stairs, but I could see María from the top already. Voluminous red hair was kind of hard to miss even with the poor light of a crescent moon peeking through a bundle of clouds.

All right, I could do this.

In hindsight, I could see where I'd gone wrong the last time. The result might've been the same, but María hadn't deserved that slap in the face, regardless of my intent. Eli shouldn't have been there, either.

Today was about fixing both those things—and, hopefully, get her back into the club. María visited Plumas almost as often as I did. She'd been there from the very beginning, volunteered to help from the start—to the point where everyone considered her a founding member, and she was in the group chat for them.

It was strange not to have her there.

My heart kicked up as I walked closer to her. I could already feel the sand getting into my sneakers. I ignored it.

"Hey, you."

María jumped on the towel she'd spread down. Watching the waves could be hypnotic, if you were into that kind of thing.

I wouldn't say I was a mountain person like León and Danny were, but beaches weren't my thing, either.

"Hey." María gave me the first real smile she'd had for me since that night. I memorized it, just as I memorized how she patted the blanket right next to her in her usual friendly way. "There's not even a grain of sand."

"I'll see about that." It was good-natured grumbling. Most people were aware of my distaste for sand. I didn't like things that got everywhere without my consent, thank you very much. I still lowered down until I was sitting next to her. "You look good."

She did.

She was wearing jeans and one of those argyle sweaters that looked extremely fluffy with a cowl turtleneck in burgundy.

"You, too." María glanced down, then looked for something in her satchel bag—an envelope she handed me. "Can you cover my membership with this?"

"Uh?"

I didn't need to grab the envelope to know there was cash inside.

"My company gave me that bonus they owed me from the holidays, but they did it in that annoying cash-only way they do to avoid paying taxes on it." She rolled her eyes. "I don't like having all those bills with me, and I can't deposit it without raising flags, so... Can you?"

I grabbed the envelope then. I wasn't a fan of handling money in public like this, but I still opened it to take a quick peak.

"This would cover... a year. More than."

María winked. "I'm good at what I do."

I wasn't doubting that. "You don't want to save it for an emergency or something?"

She scrunched up her nose. "We both know where it's gonna go if I do that."

Right. Her father.

I sighed. "I'll add a note in the server or something."

I'd have to ask Cece how to do that first. They were the tech-savvy one in the group.

"Thank you."

I frowned as I closed the envelope again. I didn't have a bag with me, but I stuffed it in the big pocket in the middle of my hoodie and zipped up my jacket. "This isn't some weird way to walk away from the club, right?"

María chuckled. "If I wanted to cancel my membership, I would've done that already."

I huffed. "That's not as comforting as you think."

"Do I have to comfort you now?"

I shook my head. This wasn't going in the direction I thought it would. It was disconcerting.

"I miss you." I turned so I was staring right at her. "And I'm sorry for how I handled things. I should've done better."

María sighed. "Kara told me you've been weird lately."

"Kara talks too much." I snorted.

I couldn't deny it, though. Kara probably didn't say weird, and she probably went into more detail, too, but I appreciated María toned it down.

"Well, yeah." Her hazel eyes crinkled at the corners. During the winter, her freckles weren't as visible, but they were still there, decorating her cheeks and the bridge of her nose. Forehead, too. "I'm not going to apologize for catching feelings or being hurt when those feelings weren't reciprocated."

My heart thrummed loudly in my chest. "I don't want you to."

It might make me a bit sick, but it was the last thing I wanted.

"I know." María leaned back, palms pressed against the towel behind her. Her gaze went back to the crashing waves before us. "I'm glad Eli is okay, and I want to renegotiate the way we play in the club at some point, but that point is not now. Not yet."

"That's understandable." I swallowed. "When I say I miss you, I'm not talking about sex or scenes, María."

I liked her in my life. She was bright and always had a smile or a laugh to spare. She had her secrets, too—secrets that made me protective of her. I couldn't protect someone if they weren't talking to me or showing up to the places where I could keep an eye on them.

"I am." María shrugged. "You Dommed me for years before I started getting other ideas. I miss it. I think I enjoyed it more, too, when things weren't tainted with what ifs and mourning what I knew would never work."

"When do you think things changed for you?"

In an ideal world, I would avoid this topic completely. I would just accept what María was saying at face value, and I would be glad that she was back to her more usual self. My head didn't work that way, for better or worse. It needed to make sense of everything. I needed to dissect and analyze every element, every choice that led to where we were now.

"I think…" María licked her lips. It was hard to be around her and not think of all the moments we'd shared, all the scenes that were now seemingly tainted because they'd meant something different to each of us. "Remember when you got those permanent markers and we all wrote on Kara's skin?"

"Yeah."

After that, I'd taken María to my office. She'd been brattier than usual and asking for something heavier. I'd made her list every reason why she thought she should be punished, until she spilled the reason why she'd been acting out in the first place. Then I'd written the punishments for each infraction over her body.

It had been a good scene. Maybe it had been more intimate than usual, but I couldn't say it stood out more than any other time. I'd checked in on her over the following days, and we'd met up for brunch the following week.

"Before that day, whenever we played or just had sex or whatever, yeah, I thought about how good you are, obviously." A dry sort of laughter followed her words. "But it was always followed by how it sucked that we weren't really compatible, that you needed things harder than I could take them, and I couldn't do high protocol long term. Or short term, to be honest."

"Yeah."

It had been the same for me. It was the same for me with most people. I enjoyed watching or engaging with them short term, but I was aware of all the reasons why it wasn't sustainable outside of the club or a particular scene.

"I think something switched in my brain that day." María glanced down. I ran the math in my head, trying to come up with a timeline. Almost a year, probably. "I don't know, I guess I was too raw, with my father's call and all that, and it meant more to me than I realized or that I was willing to share."

I nodded and tightened my jaw. "Mónica and Abel kept teasing me... warning me, really, that you had it bad for me. I'm really sorry I didn't say anything."

I shouldn't have left her hanging for a year, fostering feelings and hope for a relationship that was not going to happen.

"It's fine, Erika." María nudged my arm. It was the first time she touched me since I arrived. I hadn't realized how off-kilter things felt without it. María was the kind of person who was always touching, always looking for a hug or a squeeze. "To be honest, I don't know that it would've helped. Even if a part of me is still bitter."

There wasn't much I could say to that, so I didn't.

María took a deep breath and let it out. I watched as the wind made a mess of her curls. She only tied up her hair when she went to visit her father or had to deal with family matters.

"How are things with your parents?"

"You've only been out of the loop for a few weeks." *More than a few weeks.* I pressed my lips together before I said anything. I didn't think it worked with the way María's eyes seemed to sparkle. "You haven't missed out on that much."

"That doesn't answer my question."

If anything, it made the alarms in my head ping. Loudly.

"I'm aware." She sighed. "But I can't really get closure over my stupid crush if I run to you at the first sign of trouble, can I?"

So the alarms had been right.

"María..." I warned. I heard what she was saying. I really did. I was trying to do better, too, to not be so on top of everything and everyone. This was different. Swallowing back the words I really wanted to say left my throat feeling like I'd just chewed through a razor. "Does anyone else know?"

A couple of months ago, I was the only one she confided in about her father and everything that came from his prison stints. Right now, I couldn't tell. I hoped I wasn't.

I knew I was the second she darted her gaze away. María was easy to read, our history aside. "I'm a big girl."

"You are," I conceded. "You can still reach out to people for support."

"Like you do?" María challenged. The bite left her words, her expression, the second she realized it was out there. Her lips clammed shut before she avoided my gaze again. "Ignore that. But I've got it under control."

My ass, she did.

I kept the thought to myself. It wouldn't help anyone if

we just let the frustration grow. "Will I see you for brunch on Sunday?"

The answer didn't come as quickly as I'd hoped. It was hard to keep myself in check—to remind myself that this was progress, and it was good, and María could take as long as she needed. "I don't know. Tony is doing a workshop, though. I think I'll sign up as DM for that."

I frowned. That was… two months from now.

"All right."

"You're not going to complain?"

I snorted. "I'm trying here."

After a pause where she seemed to process my words, María gave me another of her genuine smiles. It was a victory I would take.

"We'll be fine."

"Yeah."

I would make sure that we were.

EPILOGUE
ELI

The door clicking open had my spine straightening. After a quick check that everything in the kitchen could be left as it was, I rushed to the entrance. I didn't like admitting it out loud—or writing about it, for that matter—but this might be my favorite rule.

Mistress had just locked the door when I stood there before Her. It had been raining all day. She had texted a couple of times throughout the day. Apparently, it made no sense that people stopped working out indoors because of a little rain. I knew the issue was that She'd been bored because Abel was down with a cold. She texted a lot the days when Abel wasn't there to keep Her entertained—or exhausted in the boxing ring. I was really glad that was their jock thing and not something either of them wanted to bring to their kinky lives outside of the gym.

Wrestling couldn't interest me less if I tried.

"Mistress."

All tension left my body the second Her arms wrapped around me. It didn't matter that She was cold or still wearing a coat the umbrella didn't keep completely unscathed from the water. Being in Her arms meant warmth, and quiet, and safety.

"It smells amazing here, slut."

I mewled. It only took a word and I was squirming, pressing my thighs together as all my blood rushed down there.

It did smell good.

"Thank you, Mistress." I swallowed. Sometimes hugs were a quick affair, and then I would rush to take Her coat and shoes off. Other times—like today—I lingered here, not wanting to move a muscle. "I'm making shiro and misir wat. They'll be ready for dinner."

Both the shiro and the red lentil stew took a while to cook, and Mistress's neighbor who owned the Ethiopian restaurant She liked—and who had taught me to cook both things in the first place—agreed to let me get the injera from her. Doughs had never been my thing, and I was still trying to get that one right. I knew Mistress didn't mind if it didn't come out as spongy as it should, but I'd wanted to treat Her today—more than usual.

"Can't wait."

Lunch didn't need anything done on my part, so I could soak up even more of the hug. Mistress never complained. She just held me tight and pressed Her lips against the top of my head.

"How was your day, Mistress?"

I didn't know what had me so clingy some days. Or why I needed to ramp up the protocol when it happened. Today wasn't an anniversary of anything. I hadn't heard or seen anything upsetting. I hadn't had a therapy appointment, either. The days I had therapy were the worst. I knew it was good for me, but they were draining. Kara often came over with a tub of ice cream after it was done and we would sit together for a while. I liked that she got it, and that she didn't make me focus on a screen to watch something or try to do small talk. I didn't like that I *needed* it.

I was making progress, and I was aware of that progress, but... Ash said it was fair to complain about it, so that was my excuse.

"Boring," Mistress answered. She huffed. "Bet you already knew that, didn't you?"

I chuckled. I'd just been thinking it earlier, but I wouldn't have teased her about it. I still wouldn't. "You're just impatient for tomorrow."

Mistress hummed. "Might be."

I was right.

After lots of going back and forth, Mistress had gotten a vacuum bed to be delivered to the club. It had taken Her this long because She'd wanted to have it here. I'd told her I was fine with it being for the club, but She could be stubborn. That stubbornness meant spending I didn't know how long trying to make it work before She had to acquiesce and admit the thing simply wouldn't fit here. It wouldn't match the vibe, either.

There were sex toys in the bedroom and the bathroom, but the rest of the space was... homey. To be honest, a part of me still expected to enter through the door and find a rubber-clad room full of sex machines where the living room was. It was a strange thing. Mistress had just laughed at me when I tried telling Her once.

"Let's eat, slut. I have plans for you before I go back to the gym."

I scowled. The expression lasted less than a second, but it was long enough for Mistress to catch it. Her fingers tilted my chin up, and I quivered at the hold, thighs trembling. My throat dried, heart kicking up.

"Mistress?"

"Do you have anything you want to tell me, slut?"

"No." I shook my head right away.

Whenever She held me like this, thinking became ten times harder, but everything sharpened into focus, too. I never knew how to explain it when it came up. I'd tried journaling about it, too, to no effect. I'd even discussed it with Ash. They just said it sounded like whatever it was, the only thing it brought was comfort. And then they wanted to dig deeper into why the idea of comfort made me anxious—or something like that.

My breath hitched. I didn't want to be thinking of therapy when Mistress was right here.

"Are you sure?" I nodded. Sometimes my thoughts got jumbled and I needed a second, but that wasn't what was happening today. Mistress studied me anyway, lips pursed until whatever She saw there convinced Her of it. "Good. Go grab our sandwiches, then. As much as I want you begging on your knees, food comes first."

I gasped. "Yes, Mistress."

Mistress had requested a light lunch last night. She didn't have any classes in the morning, but her afternoon was full with them, and a full stomach made Her lag or something. I hadn't fully understood what She meant, but I had leftover sandwiches in the fridge that were meant to eat cold, so I was happy to just focus on a heartier dinner. Mistress might not enjoy a full stomach before the gym, but She definitely did when She came back from it.

The sandwiches were on a tray I'd set up last night, wrapped up in aluminum. They were just a basic sandwich I made when I wanted something quick but comforting—lettuce, tomato, Manchego slices, and a dressing with mustard and lightened mayonnaise. Simple, but it made my stomach happy. Mistress liked them, too, so I didn't feel too bad about my skill as a home chef for not making anything too elaborate.

"PLEASE." I swallowed. "Mistress."

I didn't have enough air.

Rather, it felt like I didn't have enough air.

When Mistress had said the vacuum bed had arrived, I didn't know there was something else that had arrived—something else that was just for the two of us.

"Colors, slut."

I sobbed.

I didn't want to keep talking, didn't want to think about colors or anything else.

Mistress intertwined Her fingers with mine.

That made it easy.

I closed my eyes.

One squeeze.

Green.

A sob escaped as another orgasm was pulled out of me. I'd lost count of them a while ago. Mistress had said I had to keep count, and the idea of disappointing Her left a sour taste in my mouth, but there was nothing to be done about it now.

I'd just take Her punishment later and thank Her for it.

It was a long while since I'd taken a punishment. A part of me craved the utter humiliation of it—maybe the part that had led to losing count of the orgasms in the first place. It wouldn't be the first time my body betrayed me, or the first time someone told me I had to listen to it more.

The idea that I didn't listen to it was strange the first time I heard it. Now it just bothered me because I wanted to obey —and to please Mistress—more than I wanted to *listen to my body.*

"You know what is fucking with my fantasy?" Mistress groaned. She was touching Herself, out of reach from me. The mere thought had me fighting back tears. "I can't leave you like this all evening. I can't just strap you down, place a camera, and watch you writhe and beg for hours while I'm away and you're here alone with no one to help you."

But She'd planted that fantasy in my head now—on purpose, too. I knew the way She worked and the way She used verbal humiliation.

I squirmed, not that there was a lot of give.

The black straitjacket Mistress had put me in made sure of it, and the belts and buckles of the new fuck machine She'd bought kept me strapped and completely defenseless. She'd said something about how She wanted me to get used to being forced immobile.

I called bullshit, deep down—in that way I wouldn't say out loud.

Mistress might have had a point in wanting me to get that practice. Sweat built up around my hairline as I tried to buck my hips up, as my chest heaved with every ragged breath.

The fuck machines I was used to were simple benches with an engine that thrust a dildo, or two, in and out. At first glance, this one should've been the same. But no fuck machine I'd been in had as many belts and buckles as this one. The straitjacket was rendered pointless, but I liked the way the weight felt against my chest. I suspected that was the main point of wearing it—that and the aesthetics of it. Mistress was bigger on those than people realized.

I liked them, too.

That didn't mean I stopped struggling against all the holds. There was just no give. I wasn't used to being restrained, either. Most of the time, Mistress was the type of Domme who enjoyed the mind games that came from telling subs they should be able to stay still on their own. She'd often teased me—and praised me—for not needing anything to hold me down. This should be easy; it should take out that layer of... effort. I didn't realize that the knowledge that I couldn't move would eclipse all my focus. The mechanical holds meant it wasn't a matter of whether I wanted to obey or not. It wasn't physically possible for me to step away, to risk a punishment because I couldn't keep up with the onslaught.

"Open up and suck."

Huh?

I didn't give myself time to show the question floating in my brain. I opened my mouth to welcome Mistress, realizing that She had moved closer. She stood beside my head as She shoved two fingers coated with Her fluids into my mouth. I whimpered. The muskiness flooded my senses. For a long second—more than, but time quickly lost meaning in the midst of sex, sweat, and the mindset that came with those things—Mistress's fingers were all that existed. Licking them clean, even when the pressure made my throat bob, was all I knew how to do.

I moaned when She softened Her hold on me. I panted when I followed Her with my gaze to find Her lowering Herself. I'd never seen her kneel, even if that wasn't exactly what She was doing. Her knees were on the floor, but there was nothing submissive about the position. There was none of the reverence I associated with the posture.

"You're overwhelmed, aren't you slut?"

Her voice remained flat—mocking, but sweet in a way that was starting to become the norm between the two of us. It made me shudder regardless.

I whimpered.

"Do you need to use your safe words?"

No.

No, it wasn't—

pliant with the lingering aftermath the current left in its wake.

The dildo was bigger than any I'd ever taken. I was sure it was another new addition, but Mistress hadn't said, and I hadn't cared to ask.

I just cared about the burn of the stretch, the wrongness and the rightness in knowing I'd be gaping, sore, and hurting after this. I *wanted* to hurt. I craved it.

Pain was rarely the main motivator for me when I was with a Sadist. My pleasure came from the eroticism of the scene and from pleasing them. It came from knowing I was giving Mistress what She wanted, from performing well for Her and surpassing Her expectations.

"You look so fucking sinful like this, slut."

A whimper slipped past my lips.

This was what did it for me. I didn't need anything else other than Her words, Her degradation sinking down into my pores.

But this time, I needed the pain that came from being well used. I needed the exhaustion that clung to my bones after everything I thought I knew about myself had been pushed so far I didn't have a way to align everything together again—not in the same order. It was like being born again. After each scene that left me empty, I resurfaced with most of the same pieces, but not quite. They were better versions each time. The edges were more polished, the dust that clung to my bones gone and letting all the other good things seep in.

"That's right," Mistress whispered.

I couldn't tell what I'd done or what She'd seen that was worth the praise. It didn't matter.

The wand started buzzing again. I knew Mistress was moving around, making sure the positioning was right.

I sobbed as the vibrations assaulted my skin. "Mistress."

My voice sounded different. It wasn't the desperate kind of plea it had been before, when I was too in my head, too overwhelmed by everything my body was being exposed to. This was a thank you, a worship, an I'm-giving-myself-to-you-on-a-silver-platter-Mistress.

"How many orgasms have I given you so far, slut?"

I grunted.

My cheeks filled with blood. I could feel it.

"I don't know, Mistress."

The words hurt as they slid out of my mouth. But the words also had my body tensing, the warmth in my groin exploding and making me unclench with one of those peaks I'd lost count of—the ones that felt dry, hurtful even, after I had nothing else to give, but were the most invigorating too, somehow.

I didn't care too much about the logic in that. It didn't matter.

"Of course you don't," Mistress sneered.

That layer of shame, of pretend disgust in Her voice? It was the thing that kept me here, asking for more.

The machine stopped a second later. It was jarring. The dildo popped out of me almost too easily—Mistress's doing.

My hole burned, protesting the sudden void. Mistress moved Her hand there. It helped, and it didn't. The burning remained for one, two, three seconds. I didn't know. My breath hitched. Breathing helped. Slowing down my heartbeat meant the blood flow slowed down as well. It was always easier said than done.

"Mistress." It was less than a whisper.

Truthfully, I didn't know how She heard it, but when my eyelids fluttered open, Mistress was right there, watching me.

"You really are the best toy I've ever seen." Mistress shook Her head. I didn't know what She'd been thinking about. It didn't seem important. "It's a good thing, isn't it?"

I gasped. The words sunk into my skin, the praise She concealed as degradation. It was something She was doing more and more. She'd written in Her journal about it a couple of times, about finding the perfect balance that gave me the praise She'd decided I needed, without distorting everything She naturally was as a Mistress.

I wouldn't want it any other way.

"Yes, Mistress." Breathing out the assent was the most natural thing, too.

I didn't know any other way. I didn't know there was any other way. I didn't want to hear about it, either. There was no interest there.

None.

I didn't care what that said about me. I wasn't questioning things anymore—not even when Mistress Erika started unbuckling all the belts holding me tight to the machine. I might have been protesting the restraints before, but the absence of them felt just as strange. Mistress didn't give me time to get used to it, either, grabbing and handling my body until I was off the bench and standing on my feet.

My feet slipped on the floor. I didn't have the best balance while it felt like blood was still returning to my limbs, or while I was still accounting for the tingly sensations running down my body. But Mistress knew. It was why She'd made me stand up. Her mind games were not something everyone witnessed or was super aware of. They were my favorite thing about Her. I liked that it was special, something only a select few got to witness.

Just as no one else got to witness Her softer side; the side that pulled me close to Her and pressed my head against Her collarbone. Mistress kissed my temple before She started unfastening the back of the straitjacket with Her free hand. I shivered.

The absence of the straitjacket was even more disconcerting than the straps. The weight had been too comforting.

I wondered if I could convince Mistress to add it to our routines, to add one more rule. She hadn't added one of those in a... few weeks. I wasn't complaining about the pace anymore, but surely, it was about time.

I didn't complain because, unlike before, the pace now had to do with Mistress wanting me to succeed. It would be wild to find offense in that. However, I suspected a part of me would always crave more, need more. Mistress said a few nights ago that it was fine, that She liked the challenge that came with me keeping Her on Her toes.

It wasn't something I would've considered four, five months ago.

It was good, though.

"Clean up while I get ready for the gym," Mistress ordered, her lips ghosting over my ear. Her hold on me tightened, as if She needed to double-check I wasn't about to double over. "You are going to be the pups' new toy at the club tomorrow."

I squinted my eyes when She took a step back. Unsurprisingly, Her face didn't give anything away, but I still tried. "Is that my punishment, Mistress?"

I couldn't see how it would be. I liked the pups. I liked being a toy for anyone and everyone Mistress deemed.

"The punishment," Mistress said with a glint in Her eyes that forewarned what was to come, "is that you won't be able to come. And you know how insistent Cece gets when they can't make the sub they're with come."

Shit.

Yeah, I was very much aware.

"Yes, Mistress."

Mistress Erika hummed. She pressed Her lips against me. It was quick, but it was enough to make me stumble when She let go without warning. It made Her chuckle.

"I'm looking forward to seeing you cry, slut."

"Me too."

It was the only response that made sense. I'd always look forward to what She wanted to do with me. I'd always thank Her for it, for the privilege of giving Her what She commanded. This dynamic with Her meant I gave Her all the power; I relinquished every ounce of control. But, in a twisted way I'd only known about in theory, it made me feel powerful, more in control, than I sometimes knew what to do with.

It didn't have to do with gaining confidence—even if I could tell I had—or with having full awareness of the effect my submission had on Mistress, but that was another consequence of living with Her I hadn't foreseen entirely.

My knees still buckled a bit when I moved to grab the weighted blanket from the couch. I had to shower, but some days I needed to curl up with my thoughts first.

Mistress approved of it.

Anyway.

The closest I'd come to explaining it right? The power came from having a purpose—from knowing I was living as true to myself as physically possible.

I licked my lips. A shiver ran through my body.

I was home. The smell of the stew cooking in the kitchen, combined with the muskiness that clung to both my skin and the discarded dildo on the table, made it feel like home.

I didn't know until recently it was a smell I'd ever recognize if it hit me. For once, I was glad to be proven wrong.

***

Thank you so much for reading *Just One Rule*. Consider leaving a review or telling your friends about it so more people can fall in love with Erika and Eli.

ACKNOWLEDGMENTS

This book wouldn't have been possible—or as fun to write—without the support of my super fans:

- Allie
- Ana
- Giorgia
- Jordyn
- Katy

ABOUT THE AUTHOR

Hi! My name is Emily Alter (she/he/they), and I'm a queer, kinky and polyamorous author of both gay and sapphic romance books. When I'm not writing or being a brat to someone who has consented to it, I do my bit of activism as a social psychologist and licensed sex therapist in Madrid, Spain.

My writing journey began when I was a child who couldn't get enough of *Xena: The Warrior Princess* and decided to take matters into my own hands. Since then, I've become a voracious reader and a self-published author who can talk for hours about my craft, tropes, and the characters who drive all of the stories living rent free in my head.

I write in different sub-genres, and I'm always working on more than one series at a time, but a few things that always stay the same across all of my books and universes are themes of found/chosen family, sex positivity, mental health awareness, and a dash of social justice.

ALSO BY EMILY ALTER

Wanna read more kinky sapphic stuff?

Plumas Universe

Play Pretend

Just One Rule

Home Kinky Home

Mistress: Found

Multi-author series

Temptation at Randy's (Diner Days)

Dare to try adding some gay spice in there? I've got you!

Plumas Universe

Hopes and Dreams

Matching Wounds

Multi-author series

Wrestling with Daddy (Pet Play by the Lake)

Gift for a Demon (Possessive Love)

Printed in Great Britain
by Amazon